FISH

FISH

L. S. MATTHEWS

Delacorte Press

Published by
Delacorte Press
an imprint of
Random House Children's Books
a division of Random House, Inc.
New York

Text copyright © 2004 by L. S. Matthews
Jacket illustration copyright © by Jon Krause

The trademark Delacorte Press is registered in the U.S. Patent and Trademark
Office and in other countries.

Visit us on the Web! www.randomhouse.com/teens
Educators and librarians, for a variety of teaching tools, visit us at
www.randomhouse.com/teachers

Library of Congress Cataloging-in-Publication Data

Matthews, L. S. (Laura S.)
Fish / L. S. Matthews.
p. cm.
Summary: As fighting closes in on the village where Tiger's parents have been
working, the three of them and a mysterious guide set out on a difficult journey
to safety.
ISBN 0-385-73180-9 (trade) — ISBN 0-385-90217-4 (GLB)
[1. Refugees—Fiction. 2. War—Fiction. 3. Survival—Fiction.] I. Title.
PZ7.M43367Fi 2004
[Fic]—dc22
2003015385

Printed in the United States of America

June 2004

10 9 8 7 6 5 4 3 2

BVG

FISH

ONE

This story starts with the day I found the fish.

I was standing about with nothing to do, by the huge puddle I called a pond. Dad said it wasn't a proper pond, because the floody rain had left it there by accident, and it would disappear again soon.

I said, "What is it then? Because it's too big to be a puddle."

Dad had to agree I was right. He is quite tall, and it was as wide each way as three Dads if you laid them out head to toe, in a line.

At least, it *had* been that big. It had been shrinking every day since the rain had stopped, and now I realized that it had become the puddle that Dad had always said it was.

Anyway, I was standing about, as I said, with a stick in my hand poking at things, because there was nothing else to do. I couldn't swish the stick in the water because I couldn't get close enough to the edge. The mud was terrible. I had already fallen over in it three times and my clothes were covered in it. I wasn't worried about what my parents would say because they never minded, they were so busy anyway. Now that the rain had stopped, we could dry things again.

So I stood in the last patch of sticky mud before it turned into the liquid patch, and hit at some bits of green poking out of the water's edge.

All of a sudden there was a ripple and a flash, and a big fish leapt out of the brown water, making a rainbow in the spray as it flew in an arc and landed back—splash!—in the water again.

I had been feeling very gloomy a moment before. Now I stood and blinked and stared. Nothing moved. I wanted to see the fish again. The glow of the colors had flooded my eyes, like when you open the curtains on a lovely sunny day. I had a warm feeling all through, despite the mud.

I put one foot forward and tested the ground a bit further in. I had old leather sandals on and bare feet, but you wouldn't have known it. The mud had made big, oozy mud clogs around each foot.

I wanted the ground to be safe to walk on, because I so wanted to find that fish. But it wasn't safe—I knew I'd get stuck if I got any closer, and I was quite a way from the house, and maybe no one would hear me call and no one would come looking till teatime. I walked all around the edge, just in case, but it was the same everywhere.

Very slowly, because it is hard to walk in oozy mud clogs, I walked back up the rough earth path to the house.

Dad was there, because it was his turn to look after me and do the tea. He looked tired and dusty. We hadn't got much water for things like washing, in spite of all the rain.

We were a funny family—not like the ones in the books I read, which we'd brought from our own country.

That was one thing that was different about us for a start—we didn't come from the country we were living in now. Mum and Dad had brought me with them when I was little. They had come to this country to help the people, who were having a hard time.

And they *were* having a hard time, I can tell you.

First, it was boiling hot, but not like the summers in our home country. This hot was dusty hot, with no green growing anywhere. There had been bits of bushes and wispy dry grass in the beginning, I can remember, but after a while even that had gone. I had stroked the goats and the donkey who'd come to nibble at it. Then they stopped coming and I missed them and asked why they didn't visit anymore.

Mum had said, "Because there's no more grass and leaves." She had pushed her hands through her hair when she said this, and had looked so tired and sad, I was surprised. I didn't know she'd liked the animals visiting too.

The boiling hot had stayed for what seemed like forever. The people Mum and Dad taught, and sometimes helped with medicine, ran out of water and food. We were luckier, because our country was still looking after us with some food (not very nice food) and bottled water. I asked, Couldn't we give our food and water to the people?

Mum and Dad said that our country could only give enough for us really, but they were sharing as much as they could. All the people in the whole country needed food and water, and medicine, and there were thousands of them. Our little bit couldn't look after all of them.

All the same, I sneaked bits to share with my friends in the village. Most of these didn't have parents anymore because they'd been killed in the fighting in other villages. They'd come to our village because it was safe here. Some had an uncle or aunt to stay with. Lots of the women had lost their husbands and some of those women became the children's pretend mums. It probably sounds bad to you, and now I'm older, I understand better, but the fact is that all that seemed normal to me at the time and I didn't think much about it, because that was how I grew up.

Most of the kids played and teased like any kids. Some always stood in doorways with big scared eyes and never spoke. The kids who were playing might ask them to come and join in once, but when they didn't would then ignore them as boring. It was annoying when we needed an extra for some game or other. I asked Mum what was the matter with them, and she said that they'd had a terrible thing happen, or had seen something terrible. It was like a nightmare, and you know when you first wake up from it you can't just go back to sleep? They were stuck in that feeling.

So I tried a bit longer and a bit harder than my friends and one or two of those ones came round and started to play, with time, if we kept on at them. The ones who didn't I called "lost," and I felt a funny feeling like a big black stone in my chest when I looked at them, staring at nothing as we played, or rocking on the floor and growing thinner every day.

More and more of those, and some grown-ups, too, were turning up every day.

We had a ritual every morning, taking the corners of a blanket with a friend on it who couldn't walk at all, maybe with no legs. We'd pull them out to join in with whatever we were up to that day, or take them where they wanted to go. One or two of them were quite bossy, but they were brilliant at thinking up games.

One day, the rain came. At first it was exciting, and I thought everything would be better now. But although Mum and Dad laughed at me dancing in it, and came out and danced with me when I dragged them out by the hands, they still looked worried underneath, if you know what I mean.

The rain was very heavy, so heavy it hit you hard on your head and shoulders, like someone dropping a big bucket of water on you, but over and over again without stopping. You couldn't think or hear or see. Me and my friends grabbed the blankets of the ones who didn't walk and raced them back into their houses again. I sat inside and waited for it to stop. And waited.

That night, as I lay in my little bed on the floor, I heard the drumming and thrumming of the rain on the roof stop, and thought, At last. Now I can go to sleep. And maybe I can go outside and play in the morning.

But then there was a sound of people talking at the door. I could hear Dad getting ready to go out. I got out of bed and asked Mum what was happening.

She said, "The rain has come down so fast and heavily on the dry hard ground that it hasn't soaked in. It's run off and made rivers and has flooded people's homes. Dad's going to try and help rescue some of them."

In the morning Dad was on the big bed, fast asleep on top of some towels, with all his clothes still on and wet through. We let him sleep just a little bit longer, because he looked so tired, but then we had to wake him up and make him get changed and dry properly.

He sat up in bed with a hot drink and explained, "You know that big crack that runs across the top of the hill above the village where we were walking the other day, and I told you not to go near it?"

I nodded.

8

"Well, the rain had poured into it and just cut off the side of the hill—all the hill on the outside of the crack just fell away. And the rain made some of the earth into mud, and some of it was in big lumps and rocks. The whole lot fell down and covered the houses on the edge of the village. It's called a land-slide when that happens. We did get some people out. . . ." And then he stopped and just looked into his cup, and Mum said it was time for him to try and sleep again.

That rain was the rain that had left the pond. The water was drying up everywhere, and the few hungry animals left quickly ate any tiny green shoot that appeared. Instead of a dusty brown country, we were in a muddy brown country. And it started to get colder. This country was very cold at night, and cold all the time in the winter. The dead bushes were soon all gathered for burning. Trees on the hills had been cut down for firewood long ago. Dad said, if that hadn't happened, the trees' roots would have helped stop the land moving when the rains came.

en short of water before because there had
in for so long. Now everyone was short
of water, though it lay in big pools and filled ditches
all around us, because it was bad, poisonous water.
People who drank it became ill and some died. It
wouldn't be so bad if you boiled it, Mum said, but
where were the people to get firewood to make the
fires to boil it?

I was telling you how bad it was for the people here.
And if the weather wasn't bad enough, there was
some kind of war going on, though I never heard or
saw it.

"Everyone is so sick and hungry and weak. How
could they fight?" I asked Dad. He just said, "If there is
any food, or any water, the soldiers will always get it
first. They are not as sick and weak as the people we
see here every day."

So now you understand why I was gloomy, just
before I saw the fish. We'd had only some kind of
boiled porridge to eat for days now. The fact that
there wasn't very much of it was the only good thing

about it, as far as I could see, although I was hungry all the time. We followed every meal of this with a vitamin C tablet for dessert. This was the closest thing I had to a sweet, and I made it last as long as possible by sucking it very slowly.

Then my playmates from the village just disappeared one day. All the families and orphans and widows were leaving. Mum and Dad were busy in the day as never before, but more worried and serious in the evenings. They sat up late talking, talking.

"Why is everyone going? Where are they going?" I asked.

"They have heard that the war is coming here. And there is no food left here anyway. They are trying to cross the border into the next country."

"Then they will be all right?" I asked. "Why don't we do that?"

"The next country is being kind and letting them in, but they need to find somewhere proper to live. They've made a refugee camp, but it's just tents and huts. There is still not enough food, water and medicine for everyone, although the charities are sending it as fast as they can. Our people back at home have been telling us to leave for some time. We could go back there. But we wanted to stay and help for as long as there were people here that needed help," Mum explained. She looked worried, as always, but now as she looked across at Dad, there was something else in her eyes.

"Why are you looking like I do when I'm fibbing?" I said suspiciously.

Mum looked surprised and then she laughed and took my face in her hands.

"Oh, I'm telling you the truth. It's just, it's all right for me and Dad to risk staying on. And we want to do the right thing by all our neighbors here. They can't just pack it in and go home—this *is* their home. But we have to think about you, too. And staying here is not good for you. It's difficult. We hoped things would get better. We thought we could stick it out. But now it's not *if* we leave, it's when."

I didn't really follow all this, but I think it dawned on me later, when I was trudging back up the path to tell Dad about the fish, that Mum had said "when we leave," and that meant, the world was not going to be like this forever and ever, and things would be better soon—at least, for us.

When I got to the house door, Dad was stuffing things into bags. A big pot of porridge—lots of it, I noticed glumly—was boiling on the side.

"Oh, there you are! Exciting news," he said, trying to put on a pleased face over his worried one. "We're setting off back home. We've had absolutely last orders to get out. The war is coming here and anyway, the last people have left—there's no one here for us to help anymore. Don't worry, we'll have plenty of time before the soldiers start moving."

I wondered why he was hurrying with his packing so much, if there wasn't any danger, but I didn't say anything, just stood there with the mud on me sliding slightly toward the ground. He looked up from pushing a battered saucepan into a duffel bag and took another look at me.

"Oh, for Heaven's sake, look at you. Still, you may

as well use up all the water now for washing. I've packed what we'll need. There's no time to dry those clothes, that's all. Look, just leave them here. You just need clean ones on and some warm ones in your bag for the nights."

"Where's Mum?"

"She's on her way from the school hut. I've told her the news. I cooked up the last of the food so we start with full stomachs."

"Are we going on the airplane, like we came?" I asked excitedly.

"Um, no, apparently nothing's flying now," said Dad vaguely. "We are going to the border to meet the other staff and they'll fly us from that country."

"Is it far?" I asked.

"Well, quite a trek, I'm afraid. You're a good walker. You'll have to help me and your mum, I'll bet."

I hurried off to try and wash off the mud and find some clean clothes. I felt quite excited—I didn't like the sound of the walk, but at least it was a change. Then I remembered the fish—and I hadn't told Dad.

When I went back into the kitchen, Mum had turned up and was picking up things and trying to squeeze them into bags Dad had already packed.

"Leave it all, we have to carry everything on one donkey and our backs. Sit down and eat now," he said, very sternly for Dad, so that she stopped and looked at him.

I thought they were going to have one of their rows, because you can't tell Mum what to do, but to my surprise she said, "You're right," in a tired way and sat down and picked up her spoon. Dad made a face at me as if to say, "That's the first and last time she'll ever say that!" and I smiled at both of them.

In all the worry and the crossness and the hurry, there was suddenly a very quiet moment. We all sat and ate our porridge, and it was a very solemn and serious meal. When I had eaten enough—or rather, as much as I could stand—I said, "I saw a fish today."

Dad looked up, puzzled. "Where?"

"In that pond puddle thing," I said.

"Must have been a reflection in the water, or a bit of stick floating," he said, clearing away the plates.

"No, I mean, it jumped. Out of the water. It was all bright colors—or that might have been the rainbow it made when the water flew off it. And then it splashed back in again and I couldn't get close enough to see where it had gone."

"Well, it must have been a fish then," said Mum, who always believed me. "Nothing else could have looked like that. I wonder how on earth it got in there? Washed out of a river with the rain?" she asked, looking at Dad.

"I suppose so," he said doubtfully. "Shame. The water's drying up so fast."

"Then the fish will die," I said.

"All the animals here have died—and lots of the people. One fish is just one fish, after all," said Dad, as if that made it all right.

"There is water over the border, isn't there, where we're going?" I asked Mum.

"Ye-e-s," she answered doubtfully, looking at me sideways.

"We are going over the border. I could take the fish

over the border with us," I said. "When we find water, I could leave it there."

"We have enough to carry. How are you going to carry a fish?" She looked at me, amused.

"More importantly, how are you going to catch it, you silly fool?" muttered Dad as he tied up the last bag.

"If I can catch it, I can take it," I said, looking for a bucket or something to put it in.

"I never said that. Honestly . . . ," said Dad.

Mum handed me a small cooking pot with a handle. "Here you go. Somehow don't get muddy. Be quick."

"I don't think it will fit in there. It was much, much bigger—really," I added as they looked at each other.

"You will make a brilliant fisherman," said Dad. "You have the right attitude already. Hurry now—and if you get muddy, you'll have to *stay* muddy. There are no more clean clothes. You'll have to walk to the border muddy, sleep muddy and . . ."

I left them pulling the bags around to the doorway

to pack on the one remaining donkey, which a guide was bringing. Earlier, I had found it impossible to get to the water's edge. Why did I think I could catch this fish now?

Sure enough, another patch of mud in the ring around the edge of the puddle seemed to have dried up. In fact, now I looked into the water, I saw it was hardly water at all—it was almost liquid mud itself.

I poked with my stick gently, trying not to slip. For a moment, I saw nothing. Then, with another stir of the stick, a strange little black shape opened up in the thick muddy water right near my feet. A hole—it opened and shut again, like an eye blinking.

The fish's mouth! I put down the kitchen pot carefully, filled with nice, clean bottled water, keeping my eye on the muddy patch of water where the mouth had appeared.

Gulp! There it was again. Desperately grabbing for air, the fish had come up to the surface at the edge. I had no net, but somehow felt I wouldn't need it. Granddad had told Dad stories about people who tickled trout. You could just pick them up, right out of the water, if you went about it the right way.

Slow and gentle, that was it. I crouched down, very, very slowly, and slid my hands into the water without making a ripple. The water was almost mud, and it felt like putting your hands into cold soup.

Suddenly, I touched the fish. It sank away a little, but then struggled up to the surface again. I saw the open mouth, the mud-covered shape of an eye, and then my hands were around it. Gently but firmly, so it wouldn't get away, I lifted it out of the mud with both hands. It felt and looked like a huge piece of melted, slippery chocolate, but was cold, so cold. It flipped only once, in a tired way, as if it didn't really care whether I had caught it or not.

Oh, I couldn't wait to get it in that clean water. I felt I was suffocating too. As I lowered it into the pot—the fish seemed far too big, yet somehow it fitted with ease—I let out my breath and realized I'd been holding it for ages.

"There!" I said, and ran my fingers along its back

and sides under the water, to help clean it. It wriggled a bit more vigorously now, and the mud drifted down to the bottom of the pot, leaving its scales shining and bright.

I picked up the pot, because I was aching with crouching down, and carried it away from the puddle and the mud. Once on the path, I held the pot up to the light so that I could see the fish better.

TWO

Really, it was only brown, with a silver white underneath, but as it turned and moved the brown changed into speckles and spots of gold and green and even blue and red.

I carried the pot carefully up the path toward the house. It was hard not to spill the water, as the pot would swing and bump into my leg. I started to see Mum's point about the difficulties of carrying a fish all the way across the border.

When I reached the house, a stranger—not an old man, but older than Dad—was there with a little grayish brown donkey. Mum and Dad were passing bags to the man, who was expertly strapping them onto the donkey's back.

You might have said, "Surely that's too much for one little donkey to carry," which is what I used to say when I first saw the donkeys working here. But I could see that our load was about a quarter of the size of those which these little creatures normally carried.

Sometimes you would just see the huge bundles—firewood, or, recently, household belongings—coming down the street and only when they got close could you see the donkey's tiny legs and forehead and tail sticking out from underneath it all.

The donkey stood there patiently, as they do, while the man hauled and pushed the load around, at one point giving the bag on one side a shove that I thought would roll the donkey over sideways, but it just staggered a little and found its balance again.

The man turned and smiled at me when he saw me coming.

"This is our guide, who is also kindly lending us his donkey," said Dad, also adding the man's name, which I decided I would never be able to pronounce.

"Don't worry about the donkey, little one," the guide said unexpectedly, reading my thoughts. "She trusts me."

I wasn't too sure about the "little one" remark.

"They call me Tiger," I said, with my chin lifting a little.

"Tiger," he said, trying not to look surprised, "and why do they call such a little . . . why do they call you that?"

"I wasn't very big, or very well, when I was born," I said, "but Dad says I was a real fighter. Of course, I'm much bigger now. And strong as anyone."

The man had a way of seeming to look right into you, if you know what I mean—like your mother might do if you say you've tidied your room when you haven't. But his eyes were quite friendly, all the same.

"But that is not your real name," he said, with his eyebrows rising. "Your mother said you were called—"

I hated my proper name.

"You can call me Tiger," I said quickly.

"And you can call me Guide. It's easier than remembering my name," he said graciously, turning away to put a last strap in place. Once again, he seemed to have read my thoughts.

Mum and Dad smiled at each other after this

exchange between us, and Mum passed my very small bag to me. Then she saw the pot.

"Oh! I was going to say, put the bag on your back. But you—you *did* catch it?"

The Guide turned.

"What have you got there, little—er—Tiger?"

I was suddenly rather shy about my fish. I kept the pot by my side for a moment and then thought it would be rude not to offer to show the Guide, and held it out toward him.

"Oh no," groaned Dad, "it's a fish. It's my fault. I said the water would be gone soon and the fish would die, and now, *obviously*, we have to save it."

"Why, yes, of course you do," nodded the Guide seriously, looking into my pot and missing the expression on Dad's face, behind his shoulder.

"That is a beautiful, bright specimen, Tiger. I don't know that I have seen one so colorful. A little on the small side, but that is to be expected." The Guide sighed, looking around at the shabby house, the dirt track and the mud-brown, bare landscape.

"It seemed bigger when I saw it at first," I said, almost apologetically, "but I suppose at least it can fit in the pot."

"Hmm—the pot. So we need to get a lid for that, to stop the water spilling," and he turned and directed these last words toward my mother, who, under the calm, inquiring eyes of the Guide, made no more fuss, but went into the kitchen and fetched a lid that would fit.

"Will it be able to breathe like that?" I asked, as the Guide fished two elastic bands from somewhere deep within his pockets and put them around both pot and lid for extra safety.

"It is not ideal, but then none of this is," he said, casting a hand around to include the donkey, us and the whole area—and I understood him to mean this situation, his country's problems, and maybe Life, all with that one movement of his hand.

"Every time we stop, you can take off the lid and let in a little fresh air. If we have enough water, you can give it some fresh every now and then. I think," he added, taking the bound-up, lidded pot from me and tying it somehow to my bag behind my back, "I think that it will be just fine. Now, Tiger, I'll tie it like this" (here he made a noise through his teeth as he jerked something tight), "because you must have your hands free to walk where we are walking. Always remember that. What do you do when you start to fall—huh?"

"I, um, go like this," I said, and started to put my hands out.

"That's right. You put out your hands to save yourself. You also need them to hold on tight to things sometimes, or to push them out of the way. So—we keep hands free, OK?"

The Guide was talking to me like I was a soldier now, and I was pleased, so I stood up straight as I could under my bag.

"Ready?" He turned to Mum and Dad, who were looking slightly surprised by all this. It is hard for anyone to outboss Mum and Dad. To be honest, they had been so busy, bossy and tired for so long, I think they were rather pleased that the Guide was getting us all organized.

"Let's go, then," he said.

He started walking along the path that led away from the back of the house toward the road, which Dad had explained wasn't like a proper road back in our own country because it was only made of earth and rocks.

The donkey, which had no ropes about its head so was in fact loose to wander anywhere, swung around expertly and started to follow the Guide. When it came alongside him it steadied and walked there calmly like a dog. Following behind, I noticed that not only did the Guide not walk behind the donkey, as the villagers normally did, but he didn't have a long stick with which to tap it.

I hoped it wouldn't keep stopping, or we would take a very long time on this trek. I hoped it wouldn't just trot off where it fancied, with all our belongings on board.

Mum must have been thinking the same thing. "Is this a very good donkey, then, that it walks with you like this?" she asked the Guide.

"All donkeys are good, in that they'll walk like this. If we come to a dangerous bit of ground, who would you trust to find the safest way to cross—a man, or a donkey?"

Mum was caught off guard a bit by this sudden question.

"Well, I wouldn't know—people have said animals are the best. Where I come from, there are bogs—like, deep mud that you'd never get out of—with grass growing on the top so that you can't tell they're there. Local people always trust the ponies to know. . . ."

"Exactly," said the Guide, looking pleased, and leaving Mum looking even more confused.

He went on, "If I am tap, tap, tapping at this creature all the time, and beating her when she stops, and pulling her around by a rope, how is she to tell me when it is not safe to go in a certain direction?"

Dad was impressed. "That is good sense, if ever I

heard it. But tell me, won't she run off without a rope?"

"She might know where the path is safe, and where the grass is good, and a lot of other things. But she trusts me—she thinks I know more and will keep her safe. So why would she run away? Tell me, Tiger— would you run away from your parents here?"

I shook my head, looking wonderingly at him.

"No, of course not. That is good sense. It's the same for the donkey here. I feed her, I care for her, I have never let her down. Why would she not want to stay with me?"

And we all marched on over the rough earth, heads down, thinking. This was going to be a long journey, but with the Guide, I thought, it was going to be more interesting than I had expected.

There was a hissing.

I woke up from dreaming of snakes. It was dark. Blinking, and trying to remember where I was, I was pleased to find my blanket from my bed wrapped

29

around me. But I wasn't in my bed back at the house.

A very hard rock was sticking into my hip where I was lying, and I suddenly remembered. We were sleeping out in the open on the night of the first day of our trek to cross the border.

The uncomfortable rock had pushed the snake dream out of my mind. I wasn't frightened of snakes anyway, and it was way too cold for any to be out and about now. But the hissing was real.

My eyes fastened eagerly onto a glow of reddish light and followed it to the remains of the campfire. The Guide sat motionless in its glow, his khaki trousers and shirt lit almost orange against the black, starless sky. Then he reached out and pushed another few twigs into the middle of the fire and there was a crackle and a few blue flames suddenly flared orange. His shape shone white for a moment.

The hissing, I realized, was coming from Dad, still lying down, but propped up on his elbow with his back to me. He was whispering to the Guide across the campfire, but he wasn't very good at it, I thought, if it was loud enough to wake me up.

"Are you sure?" hissed Dad, just a black shape with a cold white glow about the top edge. "I really didn't want to try and cross the mountains. I mean, with a woman and child. And we're not equipped . . ."

The Guide spoke softly.

"The rumors as we left were that they have closed the border. We will not be able to cross by the road at the checkpoints. I don't care if you have papers. The border guards have their orders. The camps are over-flowing, conditions are terrible. They just cannot let in any more people. As for the woman and child, this is always what men say. Do they not shame us all with their strength in the end? Has your woman not done things you thought that even you could not do?"

And I remembered Mum working with everyone all day to help build the school hut, and then, just as everyone almost fell, rather than sat down, to eat that evening, rushing out to help a woman who was hav-ing a baby, which was stuck the wrong way up or something, and then staying up all night with one of the woman's other babies, which was sick and crying.

And then there was the time when I was quite small and I was asleep and Dad was out, and the roof over my bed started to fall in and Mum reached up and grabbed the great big timber, and held it up, and she was trying to wake me to make me move out of the way, but she couldn't reach me with her foot to give me a good kick and *still* hold up the timber. She tried shouting and everything, but still I slept on. She had told me the story and teased me about it when I was older.

"Typical you! It was terrible getting you off to sleep, you never wanted to. But when I needed you to wake up, you wouldn't!" she'd laugh.

And Dad would say, "Oh, that kid was always clever. Why bother waking up when you seemed to be hanging on to that beam all right?" But you could see he couldn't really joke about it like Mum. He still had that worried look in his eyes when he thought about it.

He'd come back, he said, and found her standing

there like she'd been there forever ("It felt like it," said Mum), still holding up the beam after nearly two hours, and he went to grab it from her and she just looked up and said wearily, "No, the child! Move the child. You won't hold it."

He decided she was right about moving the child, though obviously wrong about him not being able to hold the beam, as my mum is very small and Dad is, like I said, pretty tall, if not very wide across.

So he picked me up and moved me into the other room (and I *still* didn't wake up) and put his hands under the beam so Mum could let go, and when she put her arms down, both of them went "Oww!" and "Agh!" Mum, because of the pain as her arms came back to life, and Dad, because he could hardly take the weight and he suddenly realized what she'd been holding up.

"And it wasn't *possible* that she could," he would say, again and again.

When the men Mum had fetched had rushed in and propped up the beam with a big bit of wood (to save the roof till it could be fixed properly the next day), Dad had let go and his legs went all shaky with the shock and he had to sit down and have a drink. Mum didn't make any fuss at all, but for the next few days she couldn't lift her arms at all or move her neck very well.

With his back to me, I could still see Dad drop his head a little and knew that he was remembering this story as well.

"You're right. I just feel guilty. We shouldn't have stayed this long. Just a day or two earlier . . ."

"We can try the road, and you can show the guards your papers," said the Guide, comfortingly. "It's just we will have to walk further if it happens that we can't cross there. We can try. It is up to you. I am just here to show you the way."

I sighed at the bit about walking further. I was sure I could do it—after all, I thought about the widows and old people who'd left the village pushing my blanket friends in rickety wooden wheelbarrows, and a woman expecting a baby who had waddled slowly but determinedly behind them. But the fish? How long could it last in that little pot of water?

I turned over and looked at the cooking pot, sitting firmly on a flat rock where I'd put it when we'd stopped to camp. The lid was off, to let in the air. It was so cold tonight. I had all my clothes on, and my blankets. Did fish get cold too? Was the water frozen?

I used my elbows like a seal's flippers to drag myself over to the rock and looked into the pot. The water was just a pool of blackness. I couldn't see the fish.

"All right, Tiger?" called Dad softly, so as not to wake Mum. You could tell even in those three words that he was wondering how long I'd been awake and whether I'd overheard the conversation.

"The fish is fine," said the Guide. "If you tip the pot a little toward the fire, you'll see."

I did as he said, and the light suddenly flashed in a patch across the black surface of the water. Through it, I could see the fish. It wasn't moving around, just fanning its fins a little to keep its place. Now it just looked brown.

"Do fish sleep?" I asked the Guide.

"Of course they do, if people wouldn't keep disturbing them," he said, and I could hear rather than see the smile. He pushed another few twigs on the fire and I wondered where they had come from. No one could get hold of firewood anymore. I decided I didn't care, I was just very, very grateful. It was so cold.

I put the pot down carefully again, so as not to disturb the poor sleeping fish, and scuttled backward under my blankets to keep warm.

"Everyone should try and sleep a little," said the Guide, showing no signs of doing so himself. "We have a long way to go in the morning, and morning is not far away."

Dad lay down again, slowly and reluctantly, and I put my whole head under my blankets to try and warm up. My eyes were wide open. I worried about the border crossing. I would never sleep, I thought.

I woke up to the sound of pots clanging and a smell of porridge. It actually smelt good, which told me I must be *very* hungry. I sat up and saw the grown-ups splashing their faces with a little water from the rations and hoped they wouldn't notice if I didn't. No one said anything, and Mum passed me a hot drink and some porridge. No nagging about washing for a change—there were some good things about this trek anyway.

When I'd eaten, though, the Guide pushed a clean, wet rag into my hand.

"Just wipe around your eyes and mouth. Keep the sand off. And there are still flies in the day, even though it's getting colder."

He was right, of course. But by the time he'd shown me how to use the campfire ash on my finger to clean my teeth, I was starting to miss our bathroom.

"Do you have any children?" I asked the Guide suddenly, realizing he always seemed to know what to do, and feeling rather sorry for his children if they had to do this every day.

Everything seemed to go quiet for a moment, and I sensed Mum and Dad freezing mid-packing.

"I had four. Two boys and two girls."

"Oh," I said. I didn't like the way he'd said "had." Maybe they'd just grown up and moved away. Maybe then he *would* say, "I *had* four children." But I wished I hadn't asked.

"I lost them, and my wife, and my cousin. A missile hit the house. There was nothing left." He said this in a matter-of-fact way, as he tied another bag onto the donkey. I was relieved he didn't sound as if he was going to cry.

"But you—were you not in the house?" asked Mum.

"Yes, I was there. But I am still here. I do not ask why."

"You were lucky," said Dad, pulling his bag on his back.

"That is what people say," said the Guide, without feeling, as he concentrated on a knot, and Dad gritted his teeth, and you could see he wished he hadn't said it.

Mum put her hand on the Guide's arm and looked into his eyes. "We are glad you are still here," she said, very slowly and clearly, as if every word was very important. I can't explain it very well. It was like she was saying something simple, but meant something—well, deeper.

The Guide stopped his strap-pulling and looked back into her eyes for a moment, with a searching look. Then he gave a small smile, and a contented nod, as if they'd understood and agreed.

Me and Dad just looked at each other, none the wiser. At least Mum seemed to have said the right thing.

Having packed all the stuff together again and rubbed out the campfire, we set off along the main road again. I took this to mean we'd decided to try the easiest route first.

THREE

The first day of walking hadn't been too bad at all. But one of the things that dragged you down was the landscape.

It was boring—just dirt, dead bushes and rocks, and the mountains, which didn't seem to get closer, blocking the view ahead. Even the sky seemed to be the same brown as everything else.

We passed piles of rubble and falling-down walls, which Dad explained were old farms, small villages even. You could still make out the edges of fields and tracks, he showed me, if you looked. And here, there had been grapevines in rows—an odd stump showed, blackened and blasted.

"I thought you said the war hadn't reached here yet," I said.

"Just about everywhere in this country has been bombed and laid to waste already," said the Guide, "which is why the people were coming to our village. There was chaos here years ago—then a powerful country took charge, and in doing so, much damage was done. Then the next people took control—and they ruined anything that was left. Now they in turn are being forced out . . . so it goes on."

Beyond thinking this seemed bad and unfair, which all the grown-ups knew already, I couldn't think of anything to say, and neither could anyone else—so I frowned and puzzled and put my head down and walked in silence, with the Guide's words left hanging.

Nothing seemed to change, so you didn't feel as if you were getting anywhere. There was just the odd dead animal, tatty skin stretched like a tent over bits of old bone, dried out so it wasn't even shocking or revolting anymore. But this day showed me that there could be worse things than "boring" to deal with.

We had been traveling for only an hour or so, I suppose, when the little gusts of wind, which were freezing, started to hit me in the back harder and harder. It made you stagger. Dad turned and noticed.

"Hang on a minute," he said to the Guide, and he stopped and turned too, and the next gust of wind smacked him with a faceful of dust. While he spluttered and wiped his eyes, Dad managed to get my blanket roll from the donkey's back, trying to keep his head behind his arm to keep the grit out of his eyes.

He rigged it up around my back and shoulders, over the top of my bag with the cooking pot tied on. The blanket lashed around for a moment in the wind, but he managed to knot two corners under my chin, so well that it just about throttled me. Still, I was a lot warmer.

"This wind isn't good," said the Guide, spitting out dust. I thought, what wind would be, on a freezing cold day, with nothing but dirt to blow around?

But he went on: "It comes and it can stay for days, and get stronger. Let's move on."

Mum pulled her shawl right up over her head and kept her back to the wind. She put out her hand and pulled me closer to her as we walked, and we kept in front of Dad so we could use him as a kind of buffer for the wind.

Now my feet were beginning to get sore. They had been sore for a while, but I didn't want to complain. Dad's worry about crossing mountains with "a child and a woman" had made me determined to show him I was tougher than he thought, like the Guide said.

With the cold off my back, it was as if my body had suddenly remembered about my feet, and started to concentrate on making them hurt as much as possible. But the Guide had said we must move on, so now I couldn't say anything.

After what seemed like forever, we heard a muffled shout from the Guide, and lifted our heads, which had been ducked down under the wind. It was a change to look somewhere else than straight down at the earth road with the dust swirling round your ankles and feet, trying not to step in a pothole or trip over a rock.

Through the sandy air, we could just make out the shapes of men, some kind of bar across the road propped on old metal barrels, and a jeep. At the same moment, Mum noticed I was limping.

"What's the matter? Do your feet hurt?" she asked.

"Yes," I said, too tired to lie.

Dad nearly cannoned into the back of us when we stopped, because he hadn't heard the Guide and still had his head down. He asked what was the matter. The Guide, realizing we had stopped, sensibly backed up to us instead of turning around into the wind.

The grown-ups looked down worriedly at me and my feet, which looked fine. I looked at the ground, sorry to be a nuisance, cross at my feet for letting me down.

"We're here now, at the border," said Dad through the wind, crouching down next to my ear so that I could hear him. "Just hobble the last yards up to the soldiers. We might even get a ride from the other side of the border in a car or something. The agency knows we're coming and are going to meet us and pick us up when we tell them where we've crossed."

The Guide said nothing.

I nodded and we walked the last few yards, this time

in a line straight across instead of one behind the other.

When we reached the men, they moved across the barrier with their guns slung across their shoulders, but in a friendly way, with one walking out to meet us. Me and Mum hung back while Dad and the Guide talked to him. I noticed that the donkey, for once, didn't follow the men but stayed with us. It hung its head and looked tired.

Now the man with the gun was holding the papers that Dad had fished out of his pocket and explaining something. The other guards moved in closer to listen. Dad talked and waved his hands about.

The Guide, who had been watching but saying nothing, then had his turn. He talked and pointed back toward me and Mum several times. The first man shook his head and shrugged and talked more.

"Oh dear," said Mum, squeezing my hand.

Suddenly, the conversation seemed to be over. Dad and the Guide turned back toward us, the sand-wind hitting them in the face, but they didn't seem to care.

When they reached us, Mum set about Dad's face with a rag from up her sleeve. She looked like she was about to do the same for the Guide, but then remembered herself and offered him the rag instead. He flapped his hand as if to say thanks, but pulled out his own rag.

When they could speak again, the Guide said, "No go. Not their fault. They are soldiers. They would be in terrible trouble if they let anyone through."

"You told me," said Dad glumly.

"It was worth a try," said the Guide. "This way would have been much quicker and easier, if it had worked. They might have had orders to let aid workers through. You weren't to know. . . ."

"But now we've walked further, and have the more difficult route to follow. We could have been halfway up the mountain by now," said Dad, still cross with himself.

"In this wind," pointed out Mum.

"Let's get out of it a minute so we can think and see

about the child's feet, eh, Tiger?" said the Guide, smiling at me in spite of everything.

I felt Mum and Dad pull themselves together.

"Where's shelter? Lead on," said Dad, and the Guide nudged the donkey's neck with his shoulder, and led us off the road toward a rocky outcrop at the base of the mountains.

When you have sore feet, it seems worse to start walking again, even for a little way, once you have stopped. But I kept my eye on the rocky outcrop and knew that once there I could stop at last, so I hurried and even hopped the last few steps.

Turning in behind the first huge rock wall was wonderful. The noise of the wind didn't stop, but at least it wasn't nearly as loud, and couldn't touch us at all here. It felt as though someone had put on the heating—it wasn't exactly warm behind the wall, but it certainly wasn't so cold. I sat down on the dry rock floor and couldn't wait to get my sandals off from over my thick socks.

The adults bent as if to help and nearly knocked their heads together, but sensibly decided to leave it to the owner of the sandals (who would obviously be the most expert at undoing them) to get them off.

"Ah!" I said when they were off, and stretched out my feet in the thick socks and wiggled my toes.

"Is that better?" said Dad, amused, but the Guide didn't smile. He crouched down and carefully, slowly, began to peel off one of the socks, rolling it down from the top. I put out my hand to stop him, as there was no way I wanted to get my feet any colder—once cold, I was sure they'd never warm up again. But Mum saw something as she looked down at my feet that was blocked from my view by the Guide's hand, and sucked in her breath through her teeth.

"What?" I asked, pulling back my hand and leaning forward for a better look.

Under the sock where the straps of the sandals had been were ugly, deep red weals in the skin. "Ouch," I said, as the Guide had to unstick the sock gently from parts where the skin had oozed.

I was pleased that the damage was so impressive. You know how much something can hurt, but there's nothing to show for it, sometimes. It just doesn't seem fair. Now both socks were off, I leant back and admired my feet. I thought of the pain. Yes, my feet looked like they should if they had felt like that, if you know what I mean.

"That's a trace of mud, there," said Dad, looking closely at the damage. "Tiger! Did you clean and *dry* these feet really well before we set off the other day, when they were covered in mud from the puddle?"

"Yes, of course I did!" I said crossly. I was looking forward to plenty of sympathy for these feet, not blame.

"As well as you could, I'm sure," said Mum, digging about in her backpack for the first-aid kit and giving Dad a flattening sort of look.

"There's sand in here as well," the Guide added, to back me up, as he shook out my socks. "That has made it worse."

Then Mum said, "This will make it feel better," as

grown-ups *always* say, before they slop on something that you can guarantee will immediately make whatever hurts, hurt a lot more (at least for a moment), and I held my breath as she mopped around with stuff out of a bottle.

I managed to hold my breath until the feeling that I had just put my feet into a hot kettle, and somehow a block of ice at the same time, had passed. The pain then settled down to a nice stinging throb, so I let my breath out and said, "Thanks, that's much better," and she smiled and looked pleased.

The Guide, who had been looking at me, had to bite his lip to stop a grin. I bet he had some better medicine in his bag, probably made out of mashed-up root or something, which wouldn't have hurt half as much, but I knew he couldn't say anything, as after all Mum and Dad knew medicine, and had all the modern things in their bags.

"If I may say so," he said carefully, looking at my parents, "these feet, no matter what medicine you put upon them, should not be walked on for a while. The skin needs time."

"I agree," said Dad. "But we can't stay here for days. We haven't the food and water for one thing, especially now we are going across the mountains. Let's rest up for today and tonight, and tomorrow I'll carry you—eh, Tiger?"

No one said anything to disagree, so that's what we did. The Guide set up his fire again toward evening, as the wind roared around either side of us. The donkey huddled in close for as long as it could, but eventually started to wander out into the wind.

"She needs food," said the Guide, looking worried for the first time. "She doesn't want to go out in this any more than we do. But I don't see anything for her to eat out there anyway. I'll let her have some of her rations. She'll have to find a puddle to drink from."

Digging about in the donkey's packs, the Guide found a bundle of what looked like dead grass and pulled off a section. The donkey must have heard, even above the wind, because suddenly it peered around the rock with its large, fluffy ears stuck forward, and the sort of expression on its face that your dog makes at teatime.

We all laughed, even the Guide, and I realized that we hadn't laughed, or even smiled, for what seemed like ages. It felt so good, we all looked at each other and laughed a bit more, for no reason, and the donkey just stood and chewed and looked at us like we were all mad.

When Mum started putting the porridge ready to cook for tea, the Guide suddenly got to his feet and went off into the wind without saying anything. Dad shrugged at Mum and I thought, He's probably decided anything's better than eating that again, even dying in a sandstorm.

But in only a few minutes he was back, with a dead rabbit by the back legs. I turned away when he took out his knife but by the time the cooking was done, the smell was so delicious I was probably making the same dog's face as the donkey had earlier.

We ate, and it tasted like hot, roast chicken, and that's what I told myself it was. I didn't care if he wanted to cook *lizard*; if it tasted like this, I'd eat it. We all ate a little porridge too, to fill up on and not to hurt Mum's feelings.

Before I went to sleep I took out a cupful of the fish's water, in case it was stale, and poured some fresh in. He darted around a little, which cheered me up, and some of his old color shone as he moved in and out of the light.

"Do you think he needs food?" I asked the Guide.

"When it is so cold, no. He will manage for a few days. He has special food, where he comes from. I think if you put anything in, it will just spoil his water," he replied, and I was sure he was right.

I slept really well that night, partly because my feet were so warm. Mum had bandaged them so that they looked huge and they had a pair of Dad's socks over the top, which were the only ones big enough to fit.

In the night, I woke up again, and I couldn't think why. It wasn't a noise . . . and then I realized. It was that the noise had stopped. The roaring of the wind had disappeared as suddenly as it had arrived. Tonight, there was a moon, and the sky was inky blue and starred, instead of black.

Dad and the Guide were talking again. I wondered if the Guide ever slept. For some reason, I felt that he might be the sort of person who didn't need to—in any case, he was sensible and would surely do whatever was right. But as for Dad—if children weren't allowed to sit up all night talking, I certainly didn't think he should. I knew he did get tired if he didn't have enough sleep and hadn't he said he was going to carry me tomorrow?

Just like the first time I'd met him, the Guide seemed to read my thoughts, though he couldn't have known I was awake.

"You should rest now, and leave the worrying to me. That is my job," said the Guide. "You are going to carry the child tomorrow, you said. Why not let the donkey—"

Dad interrupted.

"No, the donkey has enough. It's my fault about Tiger's feet. I should have checked they were dry myself. I was in too much of a hurry packing, because I'd left everything too late. And I've made us all walk further. . . ."

"You blame yourself for everything. You blame yourself for even coming to this country with your family in the first place, don't you?" said the Guide, sounding tired for the first time.

"I suppose—yes, well, it does bother me sometimes," Dad muttered.

"Yet your wife told me it was she who suggested you all came here—she who made the decision."

"I'd forgotten. Yes, she did, it's true. But I could have changed her mind, I was as keen. . . ."

The Guide chuckled. "Are you sure? You could have changed her mind?"

"Well," said Dad, and he chuckled too.

"Listen," said the Guide, "you came here to help. In helping other people, you have had to put yourselves, your family, at some risk. I know why you stayed on longer than your embassy advised. You were seeing that some child had their medicine before they left for the refugee camps, that some old man who had lost his foot through a land mine had healed enough to travel. I hear about these things."

Dad looked down at the fire and said nothing.

"You came to do a job. If you had left any sooner, you would not have finished it properly. Your child has had a gift from all this that other children, staying safe in their country, will not have had." He paused, then said simply, "You cannot be other than you are."

There was a silence, and I thought that was the end of the talk for the night. I think Dad did too, because he started to lie down properly again and pull his covers up to his eyes, but the Guide started talking again, much more quietly, so it was almost as though he was talking to himself and he didn't much care if anyone was listening or not.

"You can imagine, when my family was all killed— all gone. And I seemed to be there still. Standing in the ruins of our home. Why? It must be my fault. I could even blame myself for the missile, when I had worked it all out."

I thought about Dad and the roof beam that had nearly come down on me. He had always seemed cross with himself, somehow. He had made an extra fuss of me and Mum for days, and had kept coming home early. But he had just been out working when it happened. It hadn't been his fault that he hadn't been there.

Dad put his head up again and leant his cheek on his hand and made a noise that was a kind of cross between "No, no," and "There, there."

"But that is what the mind can do," insisted the Guide. "It took me a while to realize that I had not been spared unfairly. My family were my life. My life, after all, had been taken."

Dad said nothing. Then he mumbled, "Yet you are here, now, for us. As my wife said. And I am very, very grateful." And he said the Guide's name, which I could never pronounce, and reached out and put his hand on his arm in the light of the fire.

The Guide smiled at him unexpectedly. "Yes, maybe that is why I am still here. For you."

Dad shivered suddenly and pulled his hand back under his blanket. "You are cold! Don't you feel it? For goodness' sake, put your blanket around you. For my sake, then," he added, as the Guide shook his head, smiling.

Still, the Guide dutifully reached around for his blanket and put it around his shoulders.

"And when do you sleep, man? If you're on watch, give me a shove and I'll take a turn."

"All right, all right. You get some sleep now," said the Guide, still smiling, and his words must have had a magical effect on me, because I didn't remember anything else until the next morning, when I woke to the clanging of pots and the spitting of the fire again.

FOUR

"We must thank our lucky stars that the wind has stopped, just as we're heading up the mountain," Mum said to me as she helped put the elastic bands around the fish's cooking-pot lid. "Old Fish here was the most comfortable of all of us yesterday, I should think."

When everything was ready, and I had my bag with the cooking pot tied onto it on my back, Dad crouched down and I managed to scramble up. It reminded me of when I had been really little and he would carry me around like that and pretend to fall over to make me scream.

"Just like old times, eh, Tiger?" he said. "Talking of which, don't dribble in my hair and it's a good idea *not* to hold on by putting your hands over my eyes."

Having ridden a few donkeys, I knew a thing or two and gave him a good kick with my heels just above the hips.

"Ouch! Less of that, or I might have to buck you off. Or I might wait until I find a really thorny bush. . . ."

The Guide grinned and turned away abruptly, setting off up a narrow path into the foothills, and I thought of his children and wondered if he was remembering carrying them around on his back, so I went quiet for a while and rested my chin on Dad's head.

The path quickly became narrow enough to make us walk single file. The donkey generally preferred to walk behind the Guide, but whenever we came to a difficult bit the Guide would stand aside and chirrup between his teeth, and the donkey would choose the way with a slightly reluctant look in its eyes, as if it didn't like the responsibility.

Mum chose to walk behind me and Dad, and I sensed her hovering a few times in the awkward places and knew she'd taken that position with some crazy idea of being able to catch me, or us, in case Dad fell.

But we walked out well, with Dad only gasping

slightly on the steeper parts, until we came to a place where the path divided and the donkey, who'd been in the lead, stopped and turned its head inquiringly to the Guide.

"Now," said the Guide, turning to Dad, "we can go on along this little path and it will take us to the pass, but it does get very narrow and steep and I'm not sure what condition the rains will have left it in. If we take the lower path it will lead us to a dried-up riverbed, which also leads to the pass. That is the way I would normally choose. Again, my only concern is how bad the mud will be across the riverbed."

"Do you think it will be impossible to walk along?" asked Mum simply.

"Generally, yes. I think that the rains, just for a while, made the river run again, and now there'll be mud. I would choose to walk along the raised edge, the bank. But to reach the pass, you have to cross the bed to the bank on the other side, at some point."

"So we just have to *cross* the mud, not walk along in it," said Dad thoughtfully, sliding me down off his back for a moment to sit me on a convenient flat rock. "You sound like you'd choose the riverbed."

He looked at the Guide.

"In dry conditions, it's easy. Today, alone, I would take the higher path to miss the mud. But with you carrying the child . . ." And he shook his head doubtfully.

"Might the mud be thinner or drier in places?" asked Mum.

"Well, that is the question. And that is what I hope, certainly. But it may not be easy."

"I don't see we've a choice, then—we'll have to take the lower path," said Dad slowly, rubbing his face with his hand and looking tired suddenly.

"Let the donkey take the child, now," said the Guide quietly.

"No, no . . . ," said Dad, and then looked as if he was remembering last night's conversation, and added, "Maybe a bit further on, by all means, yes."

Mum put on what I call her shut-in face, which meant, "There's no point arguing with you, I can see, but you know you're wrong," as Dad hoisted me onto his back and we set off again, the Guide showing the donkey which path we'd chosen.

This path was easier and rolled gently up and down. Now and again scruffy little blades of grass and thorny bushes with narrow leaves grew along the sides. Dad had to keep being careful not to stride into the narrow flanks of the donkey, as it would stop every so often to grab a mouthful.

Once, when it found a really tasty bush, the Guide had to scold it with a clicking noise, and Dad gave it a push from behind with his hand. The donkey gave one last jerk on the bush and took the whole thing out by the roots, and kept munching it along the way, which didn't look easy as the branches kept catching on things and getting under its hooves.

This started a chat between me and Dad about the difficulties donkeys would have in finding a take-away meal service, and the Guide listened, smiling. Dad suddenly remembered nosebags, which the rag-and-bone men had used on their carthorses when he was a boy, and the Guide was fascinated to know what a rag-and-bone man was, so Dad had to explain. He also explained what a nosebag was and asked if the people here used them.

"Oh, yes, yes. I know them. But I personally don't do that, because the food here is very dusty, sometimes moldy, and I don't think it's good for my donkey to breathe it in."

Dad said he had never thought of that, and that once again, it made good sense.

Suddenly there was a scraping sound and I had that horrible feeling like when you're going down in a lift too fast.

The feeling stopped very abruptly with a thump from below. I was still sitting on Dad's back and upright. He'd managed to fall down but land in a sitting position.

"Are you all right, Tiger?" asked Mum, with her hand pressed to her chest with the shock.

"All my insides got left behind and then they came back up and smacked the top of my head," I said, because it was the truth, and to my surprise the Guide and Mum seemed to find this funny.

Then they looked worried again, and started asking Dad if he was all right too, and Mum hauled me off backward, which was easy because my toes were on the ground anyway, and the Guide put out a hand and pulled Dad to his feet.

"I know exactly what you mean, Tiger," he said, dusting off his trouser seat and glaring at the Guide and Mum. Someone should tell grown-ups that putting your hand across your mouth doesn't hide the fact that you're giggling.

Then my heart gave a thud.

"Is Fish all right?" I asked Mum urgently, showing her my back.

"Yes, not a drop of water spilt. He's hanging a bit lower down now, but he's still on," she said, as she brushed Dad down to show she did care really, even if she had giggled.

"I was talking too much, and not concentrating," said Dad.

"Oh, talking makes the distance shorter and the way easier," said the Guide. "It takes a while to learn to concentrate at the same time. You'll soon get used to it. Only a little way to go, and we reach the riverbed. The bank at least will be dry and we can stop and rest and eat. Then maybe you'll think about using the donkey," he added, looking at Dad meaningfully.

Dad didn't say anything, but picked me up again and we set off along the track again with me gripping a little tighter than before, and the donkey rather irritated that it'd had its surprise snack break interrupted again.

Soon the path dipped down and widened out, ending at what had once been the bank of an old river. As we came to the end of the path, a large, dark bird took off from somewhere on the scrubby ground and flapped away low over the bushes, with slow beats of his shabby wings as if he didn't intend to go very far.

Because of the rains a few tufts of grass grew, some on tussocks that had been swept down when the land had given way further up the mountain. Here and there, boulders and dead bushes and old tree roots lay strewn about.

What a mess! I thought. It looked exactly as if a giant's child had been playing in a sandy, muddy corner of his garden, and no one had cleared up afterward.

But what everyone stared at was the riverbed itself.

Beneath a cold, colorless sky, a sea of mud stretched wide across, wider than anything I would have called a river. I looked across to the far bank. It looked miles away. Bushes were just little dots. It looked impossible.

In the silence, as we stared, the sound of buzzing flies drew our eyes to the rotting carcass of a goat, which must have been swept down by the rains. The donkey snorted sharply through its nostrils and backed away and shook its head. Mum, Dad and I looked first at each other and then at the Guide.

"Rest and eat, then think," he said.

Sometimes I wondered if the Guide had learnt the things he said as sayings from his mother—you know, like, "A stitch in time saves nine"—or whether he just spoke like that and made them up as he went along. I didn't dare ask him, in case it was a Personal Question.

Mum said it was rude to ask Personal Questions, and I was never quite sure what that meant, except I knew it applied to eyepatches, because that's when she'd brought up the whole subject.

I had asked a visitor, a smart old man who was supposed to be someone quite important, if he was a pirate, as he had an eyepatch, and even then, I think Mum may have got it wrong about this being a Personal Question, because he didn't seem to think I was rude, and laughed quite a lot.

We didn't much feel like resting here, or eating, with the goat and everything, but we moved further down the bank onto a place where the giant's child had kindly placed the boulders like seats around a cleanish, flattish area for our donkey and packs, and settled down. We didn't light a fire, as the firewood had to be saved for nights.

Dad dug out a tin of some kind of mashed-up meat he'd been saving, and it sounds horrible, I know, to eat it cold out of the tin, but it didn't taste too bad. Then Mum mixed up sugary powder out of little packets with the bottled water and we all drank some, except the Guide, who just drank his water as it was. The donkey was fine, because it had the tussocks of grass and leaves from the bushes. But I saw Dad looking at it thoughtfully, and realized he'd noticed that the most tempting grasses were right on the edge of the mud, and the donkey, whilst desperate to reach the blades, was very cautious about where it put its hooves and was stretching as far as it could with its neck without stepping off the dry bank.

While we were watching the donkey and Mum was packing away the empty packets and water bottles, the Guide was pacing up and down the bank. I thought he wanted to find somewhere narrower to cross, but it looked the same in all directions as far as you could see.

Then I noticed that he was looking at the banks and the mountain on either side of the riverbed. He saw me looking at him.

"I'm looking at the way the land goes up and down," he explained.

"We call that the lie of the land," said Dad.

"Yes, that's it, exactly. The lie of the land," said the Guide, trying out the phrase and liking it. "I can't see through the mud, but I might be able to work out where it's likely to be less deep. We need sticks," he added, whisked out the knife he'd used for preparing the rabbit, and started choosing branches from the bushes.

When he'd cut them I looked at them, disappointed that I wasn't going to have one. Stupid feet! Why did I have to be carried? I considered myself an expert on mud, after the puddle at home. I was sure I'd be better than Mum and Dad, at any rate.

"Are they long enough?" I asked.

"If a stick this long doesn't touch the bottom, we don't want to go there," said Dad firmly, and I realized he was right.

"The child on the donkey?" asked the Guide again, but without much hope in his voice.

"Donkey has the packs and is going to show us the way, isn't she?" asked Dad. "Adding the child will put her off balance and make her sink more."

I quite liked riding donkeys, and I thought that the Guide always knew best. I was also not looking forward to hanging on if Dad slipped again, though if he managed to fall the same way as before, I was satisfied that I'd probably stay pretty dry, although Dad might go under.

The Guide, unusually, started to chivvy the donkey around the bank, to show her that we really had to cross. The donkey thought it would be a far better idea if we just followed this bank, where the ground was safe and dry, but finally got the message.

She went backward and forward, putting a front hoof in here, and trying another there, her ears stuck hard forward. She slowly narrowed down an area about two feet of bank wide. Then she did some more checking and sideways shuffling, and took quite a bold step out into the mud. Soon she was walking, and the mud only came up to just above each hoof.

Dad said, "Clever old thing. I wonder how that system works?"

"It's like she can see through the mud," I said.

We took up our old positions again, but this time I felt it was Dad worrying about Mum, instead of the other way around. He kept stopping and trying to look back at her, but couldn't really keep his balance and turn with me and my pack on his back and both of his feet in the mud.

"You look straight ahead, Dad, at the donkey and the Guide, and I'll keep checking on Mum," I said at last, and he said:

"OK, good idea."

The Guide called back, "Stay close together now. We must follow *exactly* where the donkey treads—not a little to the left, not a little to the right. I will follow her exactly, you follow me exactly, and the person behind you does the same. Use your stick all the time to the front, to both sides, before you take a step."

The mud became deeper—up to Dad's knees, and higher on Mum, who is smaller. But we were getting across. It was taking ages, however. After what seemed like an hour, we were only a little way away from the bank we'd left. Checking before every step slowed us all down.

Dad must have wanted it over quicker than all of us. Once out in the mud, there was no way he could put me down to take a rest.

I started telling him about my design for a mud boat or raft, remembering what the Guide had said about talking being good, and Dad thought of lots of important ideas that might help stop it from sinking.

"Ho!"

The Guide stopped and raised his arm suddenly.

We looked up. The donkey, who had no stick, but, like us, was somehow checking every step before taking it, had stopped.

None of us said anything. We didn't know how her special powers worked, but she certainly looked like she was thinking, or listening, and we did know it's easier to do that if people aren't chattering.

The donkey cast her head and neck side to side for

a moment. Then she just stood, as if she had given up the job and now it was someone else's turn.

Carefully, the Guide waded up to the donkey's hindquarters, and staying close to her side, felt along her back until he reached her head.

He reached with his stick into the mud in front of the donkey—this side, that side, a little further. Our hearts sank as we saw the stick disappearing.

"Oh no, I think that means we'll have to reverse a bit," said Dad, jockeying me up a bit higher on his back.

The Guide moved sideways from the donkey's flank now, parallel to the opposite bank and pointing up-river, feeling every step of the way with his stick. The mud was too thick to swish the stick through it. You had to put it in, draw it back out, and try again.

He was very patient, but I was starting to get frightened for the first time. If we gave up and turned around, would we even make it back to the bank now?

The Guide had found safe ground. He moved along it several feet, and the donkey, encouraged, picked up her heavy head, turned sideways and began to follow. Then the Guide managed to find a shallow enough place to start heading straight on toward the opposite bank again, and the donkey set off quite confidently, so the Guide could take up his position behind her again.

Mum and Dad each traced the maneuver with their own footsteps. Then, before we knew it, me and Dad almost trod on top of the Guide as the donkey had stopped suddenly again.

"Oh no," groaned Dad for the second time. But the donkey thought for a moment and then moved sideways and started to stretch for a branch with a few leaves on it that was lying on the surface of the mud.

"*That's* why she stopped. No you don't, you cheeky devil," and before anyone could stop him, Dad sloshed and slurped his legs across to head the donkey off before she could reach the stick.

It was as if Dad had just stepped straight into a big hole. There was the horrible dropping-down sensation again and the surface of the mud seemed to rise up to meet me. This time, the sinking stopped with less of a thud than when Dad had fallen on the path. The mud was level with my feet and his waist and Dad had managed to stay upright.

No one moved or said anything for a moment, and Dad stood very still, hardly breathing. The donkey looked puzzled for a moment and then reached for the branch anyway, dragged it across, and nibbled the leaves off while everyone looked at me and Dad.

"What was all that about, eh?" said the Guide, sounding cross for the first time. "Stand still, now, stand still," he called, as if afraid of what Dad might do at any moment. I could feel Dad standing stock-still with shock, so I could have told the Guide he wasn't about to rush off.

"I think I'm stuck anyway," called Dad, over his shoulder, because his back was to the Guide, who was floundering toward us. I turned and looked at Mum, who was hurrying in our direction too, but remembering to be very careful to test the ground with her stick, as the Guide had told us.

When they reached us, the Guide managed to turn Dad around to face him, and took both his hands, which was difficult, as both of them were also keeping hold of their sticks. Mum planted herself firmly to one side of the Guide and made as if to lift me off, over Dad's head.

"No, no, you will just fall forward with the weight and both you and the child will be in the deep mud as well. Take a hold of Tiger's backpack straps, and pull toward us when I say," said the Guide.

I didn't like to hear his voice worried and irritated. Nothing had bothered him up till now. I took it as a bad sign. We were not going to make it out of this.

With the Guide and Dad grasping each other's fore-arms, and Mum gripping tight to my bag straps in front of my shoulders, Dad said:

"OK, ready, *pull!*"

Three things happened at the same time:

Mum and the Guide each gave a tremendous pull.

As we lurched forward, a huge, tatty bird swooped low across my head as if from nowhere, and I ducked and screwed up my eyes and maybe, I admit, screamed.

At the same time, there was a dull ping from the bag on my back, and a muddy splosh from behind me. I was still on Dad's back, but with the combined efforts of Mum and the Guide he managed to move back to safety.

As Dad's feet landed on the safe ground alongside Mum and the Guide, so that he was only knee-deep again, I shrieked and twisted round to look behind us.

"Steady, Tiger, you'll have us in again!" cried Dad.

"But the Fish! The Fish! Mum!"

The cooking pot had landed on the surface of the deep mud, and was sinking rapidly.

You never know with Mum. For all my frantic shrieking, I still didn't know if she realized how important it was to save the Fish. She might well have said, "Oh for goodness' sake, Tiger, you and Dad might have been killed. Stop going on about a fish!"

But she darted her arms out to grab the pot, not taking a step from the safe ground, and grabbed the string tied to the handles. She pulled, but the string was slithery with mud, and her hands flew off. The pot was still sinking.

She bent down further and grabbed both the pot's handles and pulled.

"It's stuck! I don't believe it! It's stuck faster than you or Dad!"

"The Fish! Save the Fish!" I screamed now, despairing.

Mum said afterward that it was those words that gave her the idea. The pot had sunk further until the mud was almost over the lid. Scrabbling at the elastic bands with her thin fingers, Mum got them off and pulled off the lid, with a great slurping sound from the mud. In the same gesture, she flung it away wildly. As she isn't great at throwing, it landed smack! near Dad, and splattered our faces with mud.

She had her hand in the pot, as the mud flowed in and over the edges. Out came her hand as the pot disappeared from sight.

"Did you get it? Did you get the Fish?" I screamed, still wild, not daring to believe she could have.

The Guide had watched all this unfolding from his position facing me and Dad, where he could not quickly get by to help. But he had realized Mum's plan and as quick as a flash, had one of our little water bottles in his hand, half full.

"Here!" He took off the lid. "Put him in here!"

Surely he would never fit. The Fish was far too big to fit through that tiny hole that was the mouth of the bottle.

With another of her deft movements, Mum's hand was over the neck of the bottle, and "There!" she said.

"Is he . . . how could he fit?" I asked, as they all reassured me and Mum held up the bottle so that I could see the Fish, swimming worriedly around in his smaller world.

"He—he looks smaller," I said, worried but relieved. "Fish can't shrink, can they?" I asked the Guide.

He didn't answer that one.

"It is lucky he *is* small, anyway," he said, "or he would never have fitted in the bottle."

"Have you finished screaming now, Tiger?" said Dad, who had been forgotten in the drama and was facing the wrong way to watch the rescue. "Only I think you may have deafened me forever."

I was a bit embarrassed about my panic over the Fish now, but I was still glad he was safe. "Er, yes, sorry."

"Some people might have thought it would have been more reasonable to make all that fuss when *we* were in danger," he added.

Then he said to the Guide, "I'm sorry. It was lucky I didn't kill us all. Donkey knows what she's doing. I think Tiger would be safer on her back, if she would be kind enough. . . ."

"That's fine," said the Guide, looking relieved.

"I'll take my pack from her back, in exchange," said Dad, and untied it and put it over his shoulders, as the Guide lifted me across the mud and sat me almost on the donkey's shoulders, in front of the packs.

"Hold on back here," he said, taking my hands and firmly wrapping them around two of the straps behind and either side of me. "Then if her head goes down, you won't slide down her neck and off the end."

"OK. Thank you," I said.

"And try not to scream in her ear," added Dad.

FIVE

Nothing else dramatic happened during the crossing. I balanced on the jutty bit between the donkey's shoulders that they call the withers, and felt quite lucky at first. By the end of the crossing, I felt as if I'd been balancing on the crossbar of someone else's bicycle for hours, and I never wanted to sit on a donkey again.

Mum, Dad and the Guide dragged each leg painfully through the mud. Dad said it was like walking through treacle—in fact, now he came to think about it, he had had nightmares like this.

Everyone then remembered that they'd had nightmares like this too, and we all compared dreams. That passed the time a little. I said, I wondered if donkeys had nightmares, and if our donkey had had the same one about wading through treacle or mud.

"If she hasn't before," said Dad, "she probably will have from now on."

The mud became deeper when we reached the middle of the riverbed, and I pulled my feet up on either side of the donkey's neck, and started to worry about everyone, particularly Mum, because on her the mud was almost up to her armpits.

But she called out that the mud was much thinner and more watery here, so it was easier to get through.

The second half of the crossing went slowly at first, as the mud grew shallower but then thicker again, and now everyone was so tired. But as the bank approached, my heart started to well up with excitement. I had got used to the feeling that we were trapped in this crossing, and would be doing it forever and ever. The bushes on the bank grew larger and larger, and the faint green of the grass tussocks grew clearer and brighter. Soon I could even see the leaves on the bushes, and the blades of grass. I realized that when we reached the bank, we would be out of this mud at last.

The donkey must have had a similar feeling, or maybe it was just that the grass was looking the way a table laid with food must look to us, because she picked up her head and feet and started to hurry, until she was almost trotting as we left the last few feet of mud and clambered onto the bank.

The Guide, Dad and Mum trusted the donkey's instinct, dispensed with checking the last few feet, and rushed after her. Soon, we were all on dry land again, which was as well, because the dull sky was becoming duller as night drew down from the mountains.

Dad lifted me down and started to shiver. All of them were caked in wet mud, and with the evening came the cold. While Mum and Dad got dry clothes out, the Guide, having quickly scraped some of the mud off himself with his stick, didn't let them change until he'd got the fire going—which was a good idea, because I think they would have frozen if they'd tried to undress and dress again in that cold air.

"I know you don't like the porridge, Tiger," said Mum, "but there's nothing else and I think we need something warm in our insides tonight," and she started to prepare it, but Dad took over because she looked so tired.

"I'll just look for a rabbit or maybe a bird, too," said the Guide, to cheer me up. "But I don't think there will be much around here."

I had to agree with him. If I were a bird or rabbit or, come to think of it, just about anything alive, I would try and find somewhere else to live.

While the porridge was cooking Mum carefully took off my socks and bandages, which was wonderful because my feet were becoming itchy and it was maddening because I couldn't scratch.

"Best get some air to the skin now. It's the only chance you'll have to have bare feet, while the fire's lit. They do look better!"

I admired my almost repaired feet as I stretched out my bare toes to the fire and wiggled them.

"Does that mean I can have my socks back now?" asked Dad hopefully, and sprang on them and dragged them on when Mum said yes.

We had started to eat the porridge by the time the

Guide came back. Dad jumped slightly, because he just appeared without a sound.

"I am sorry. I can find nothing," he said, and sat down gratefully and took a bowl of porridge from Mum.

We all made noises of thanking him for trying anyway when he must be as tired as the rest of us, and I tried to eat my porridge but couldn't manage very much.

My stomach ached, in an empty, hungry way, but somehow the porridge only seemed to make it ache more after a while.

We were all so tired that we lay down straight after eating and pulled our blankets around us to sleep. Even the donkey, who had been cheerfully tucking into the sparse greenery as though she would never stop eating again, propped herself with one back hoof resting under her, and sank her head low, her eyes blinking and almost closed.

That night, something strange happened.

My stomach must have been hurting so much in

my sleep that it finally bothered me enough to wake me up—at least, I thought I was awake. I could hear a slight whimpering sound, and when I came to a bit more I realized to my surprise that it was coming from me.

I quickly bit my lip, because I didn't want to wake the others—even the Guide seemed to be sleeping tonight. But another pang hit my middle, and in spite of everything, I groaned again.

Tonight, there was a moon, and the light glowed whitely along the edge of the bank I was facing. The glowing embers of the fire warmed my back. Suddenly, I sucked in my breath. On the bank stood a wolf—or a wild dog—looking straight at me.

Its coat, I suppose, was dark gray, but lit by the moon, it glowed silvery white all round. Its shadow was huge, and close enough to fall near my backpack, which I was using as a pillow. I glanced instinctively at the little bottle of water on the rock next to my head. The moonlight shone in through the clear plastic, and the Fish, for the first time on the journey, darted around cheerfully, with tints of all his beautiful colors shining in the light as he turned this way and that.

Then I looked over at the donkey. She dozed still, but had one eye fixed calmly on the visitor, and one ear tipped lazily toward it.

I felt the eyes of the creature on the path still fixed on me and looked back at it.

The eyes were very pale gold, the pupils just thin, black slits.

In one movement, it put its head down and picked up something I hadn't noticed that had been lying near its front paws. It took two paces closer to me—still, I didn't feel afraid, I don't know why—and dropped the something with a light thud about a foot away. Then like liquid, the creature turned and was gone, melting into the night and the unlit scrub.

I pulled myself up on my arms, not wanting to come out from under my nice warm blankets, and inched closer to whatever it was the creature had left.

It was a rabbit, unmarked, but unmistakably dead.

Not sure if I was really awake, I decided that this

was a dream, and best left for discussion in the morning. I crawled back under my covers and went back to sleep, even with my aching stomach.

Next morning, I felt a hand shaking my shoulder. It was the Guide.

"Tiger! Where did this come from?"

"You have not been sneaking off and hunting alone at night, have you?" asked Dad.

Mum said irritably to him, "Don't be—" then changed her mind and said, "Mind you, I wouldn't put anything past Tiger."

I sat up, rubbing my eyes and a bit cross, as would you be if someone woke you up like that. "What are you talking about?"

The Guide asked more gently, "Don't you know how this rabbit got here?"

"Oh, it's still here?" I asked. The grown-ups looked even more confused.

"I mean, I thought it was a dream," I explained. "The wolf brought it."

"Wolf!" said my parents both together.

"Or dog thing. I don't know."

Both of my parents looked at the Guide. He shrugged.

"Wild dogs, there are plenty. Wolf—a few have returned, so they say, to this area. Some of the wild dogs look so like wolves, it's hard to know the difference. They can breed together."

"I wonder why it just left the rabbit," said Dad. "Perhaps it was startled to find us here and dropped it."

"I don't see why it should drop it before it ran off," I said. "And I don't think it looked startled, exactly. I was groaning a bit, I suppose that might have—"

"Groaning?" Mum said, "Whatever for?"

"In my sleep. Well, and when I woke up. I had a tummyache."

"I wish you'd tell me—" began Mum, looking worried, but Dad interrupted her. He looked as though a thought had just struck him.

"When you say groaning, Tiger, could you have possibly been more like, well, whining?"

"I don't whine," I said stiffly, and in the pause that followed this statement the adults looked at me intently. I thought for a moment. "Well, I suppose it might have been a bit like whining."

"I just wondered if she was carrying food for her cubs. Maybe she'd even lost them. People have claimed similar things have happened." Dad looked at the Guide.

"Certainly, all the females share in looking after one family of cubs. If the mother dies, another will become the mother. It's true that if this one had heard the—excuse me, Tiger—whining sound—she might have taken it for a cub in need of food."

"Well, she wasn't far wrong there," I said.

"This is true," said the Guide, "and why do we question what has been given, when it was needed?"

"That's a point," said Dad cheerfully. "Ours is not to reason why, and never look a dead gift rabbit in the mouth."

The Guide, who was picking the rabbit up by the back legs and drawing his knife, stopped and looked so puzzled at this that Dad had to explain the true saying to him, which he thought was a really good one. He became very cheerful too, and said there was plenty of firewood here on the bank, and we deserved a really good breakfast after yesterday.

Then, thankfully, he took the rabbit away to deal with it, and Mum and Dad sorted out the fire, so that I could get up in a bit of peace.

Hot roast meat is a strange sort of breakfast, but at the time it tasted like the best one I could remember eating, ever.

There wasn't very much—one rabbit doesn't go far between four people, and this one was skinny as there was so little food here for it. But we all went quiet and concentrated as we ate, and I made mine last as long as I could, and then we all licked our fingers before having a few swigs of water each, and packing up the things again.

It was good to put on my socks and sandals again, and set off on foot like everyone else. As the Guide set off ahead of the donkey, upriver along the bank, Dad turned to me and said, "All right, Tiger? It's up the mountain today!"

"Yep," I said, "I'm good at climbing."

"Good," called back the Guide, "but don't worry, we are using the pass and it is narrow in places, but not too steep after the first part."

Just then, there was a distant bang, a pause, and then another. The Guide stopped and listened.

"Is that thunder?" asked Mum, looking at him, and then at the sky, puzzled. It was colorless and cold, as ever.

The Guide didn't say anything, but stood grim-faced, listening. We were all quiet. I could see from Mum and Dad's faces that the grown-ups, as usual, were all in on something, and I didn't know what.

"What is it?" I asked, and at that moment there was another dull bang, from somewhere way behind us, and a nasty, sharp, repeated crack, crack, like a firework.

"The fighting has come," said the Guide simply, and the look on his face was not of fear, but sadness.

"Will they . . . I mean, will we . . . ?" I asked urgently. I didn't want to be in a war. I had seen the people with bits missing, whom Mum and Dad had helped in our village.

"Their war is down there, not up here," said the Guide reassuringly, waving his arm in the direction we'd come from.

"Are you sure there won't be soldiers up here?" I asked.

"Fighting men, maybe, I wouldn't call them soldiers," he said. "Some are hiding in the mountains. But they have no quarrel with you and your parents. Don't worry." And he turned and walked more quickly along the bank, the donkey jogging to catch up, and Mum and Dad and me hurrying behind.

We walked in silence for a while, listening to the terrible sounds behind us. I kept reminding myself, Everyone has gone, everyone has left. They can only blow up the huts and houses. But then I thought of the rough little house that we had called home for so long, and the things we'd had to leave behind, and the school hut Mum and Dad had helped build, and I felt a lump in my throat. Looking at Mum, I realized she must have been thinking the same thing, so I caught up with her, held her hand and gave it a squeeze.

Mum is really very pretty, but now I saw that her hair, which is usually shiny and dark, stuck to her face in dusty strands, and her eyes looked tired and old. There were pale streaks in the grime on her cheeks, and I realized with a shock that they were made by tears.

Mum absolutely never cried. Even now, you wouldn't have known it. She sniffed a bit, and her nose went a bit red, but she kept on walking without making any other sound.

I looked back at Dad, and he must have seen something in my face, because he came up alongside us, put his arm around Mum's shoulders and gave her a sort of sideways hug. That made her stagger and nearly lose her footing, so that she hit his shoulder and they laughed a little.

By now, we had tracked to the right, away from the

bank, and were onto a proper path. As this climbed, it grew narrower.

We all pressed on, especially when the Guide called back, "We can be at the top before nightfall, if we keep moving."

"And then it's all downhill from there," said Dad, and called forward to the Guide: "Do you reckon a day for coming down the other side?"

"Yes, yes, less than that. But the downhill part might be trickier."

I didn't see how, and our spirits rose. Maybe only one more night out in the open, with our vitamin C tablets and porridge and mouthfuls of water.

Up, up we went, and I was hardly bothered that my sandals were starting to rub the old sore patches again. After the good breakfast we'd had, we decided not to stop for lunch—we hadn't much food left, and the path was becoming so narrow, there wasn't really anywhere to camp.

"It flattens out on the top," the Guide called back, "so there will be a place for the fire tonight."

We had come to the narrowest part of the path so far, so that you almost only had room for one foot in front of the other. There was a scrubby, sheer drop to the right, where the mountain plunged down into what looked like a bottomless gorge, and another, larger mountain loomed up beyond that. To the left, our mountain continued up, higher, above the path. The rocky outcrop, dotted with a few bent bushes, nearly knocked your shoulder as you passed. I found it easier going if I didn't look down.

I looked ahead to see how the donkey managed. She was now in the lead, as the safest one to check the way for us.

Under the packs her little rump was, I saw, narrower than any of us, except maybe for me. Her hocks almost bumped together, and her hooves were tiny, tip-tupping along on the hard rock.

"Maybe your wolf will bring us something else for tea tonight, eh, Tiger?" said Dad, always a big eater, and missing lunch more than the rest of us.

Suddenly, I saw the donkey tilt her head sideways,

roll her big eyes and jump to the right with all four feet at the same time. I just had time to glance up at the rocky outcrop to see what had startled her, before I realized that she was almost over the edge.

Her front and back hooves on the right-hand side slithered off the path. Frantically, she managed to twist so that both front hooves were on the path, but in doing so lost her other back hoof over the edge. Her back end swung out over the gorge, so that for a second she seemed to be only touching the ground with her front feet. She let out a bray of fear.

We froze for a second. Then, as the dust whirled and the loose pebbles bounced away down the gorge, we realized that she was still there. Somehow, just the toes of her back hooves balanced on a jutting edge of loose rock.

The Guide rushed to her head, but there was no rope to grab. Instead, he threw one arm around the trunk of the nearest bush, which clung perilously to the edge of the path in the thin soil, and the other arm around her thin neck. He had her, but she wheezed and gasped, whether in fear, or because the Guide's viselike grip was throttling her, I didn't know.

Mum seized her spiky forelock, as she would have led a pony back in her home country, and braced herself on the path, but the Guide said urgently, "No, or at least, take the bush with your other hand, or she will take you over when she slips again."

I didn't like the "when" instead of "if." Mum and the Guide had the donkey, for the moment, but there was no way they could pull her up, and no way the donkey could pull herself up, with both hind feet balanced on rubble that would give way at any moment.

SIX

Dad, who had been standing thunderstruck, seemed to give himself a shake. "It's the packs," he said, darting over to the Guide and fumbling for his knife in its sheath at his side. "She could get up if it wasn't for the packs."

The Guide said nothing, but held desperately to donkey and bush. More stones slid away with a hollow rattle, down into the gorge. The donkey stood, tense all over with the effort of balancing, her eyes wide with fear and her mouth open and gasping.

Mum said, "But . . ." and then fell silent.

Dad sat down on the edge of the path by the donkey's front feet, and his fingers felt along an old tree root. It curved out and back into the soil again like a perfect handle. He pushed his left hand between it and the rock, and gave a good pull. It seemed to hold well enough to satisfy him, and, crouching down, keeping one foot on the path and one just below the root, he reached up with the knife in his right hand and slashed and sawed at the straps holding our bags.

The Guide's knife must have been very sharp. As quick as a flash, one after the other, the bags fell and crashed away down the gorge.

"Now!" said Dad, backing up and reaching the path, and he seized a handful of the donkey's mane, and one of her ears, disregarding the advice about holding on to the bush, and all three of them heaved.

The donkey realized what was going on, made a desperate effort with her shoulders, and managed to get her back feet onto the edge of the path in one bound, almost treading on her front ones. She made one spring forward and was safe, Dad leaping out of her way in the nick of time, with the Guide and Mum almost knocked flying.

No one could speak for a moment, but coughed and gasped, and banged the dust off themselves, while I just stood as rooted to the spot as I had been when the donkey had first shied. The whole thing must have been over in a few seconds, but it had seemed like a lifetime.

"Well done, that was very well done," said the Guide to Dad. "I would not have acted quicker. Only you had the arms long enough to reach so far. But your packs . . ." And concern crossed his face.

"If the donkey went, all the packs went too, anyway," said Dad. "Better save the donkey and at least half of our stuff." He tried to sound matter-of-fact, but tried a bit too hard, so we all realized at once that he had really only thought of saving the donkey.

Parents are so strange. You would have had Mum down for the animal lover, as Dad didn't seem to be too interested in them, to be honest. But he had grown fonder of the donkey than any of us, except maybe the Guide—though he wouldn't admit it.

We all looked at him, the Guide puzzled, and me and Mum surprised, and then Mum laughed and threw her arms around Dad and gave him a big kiss, and then did the same to the donkey. I'm not sure anyone else had done that to the donkey before, but she seemed not to mind and perhaps even liked it.

The Guide's smile disappeared as he turned to examine his previously expertly tied load, or what was left of it. The donkey now had bags only on one side, but still had the cut straps attached, so he could unload her and redistribute the weight evenly. This was very difficult on the narrow mountain path. The Guide battled to tie on the bags with his back to the rocky outcrop, when there was really only room for either donkey or man, but not both alongside each other. Understandably, the donkey seemed nervous of standing on the edge of the path, and pressed against him.

Eventually, however, he managed.

"We've lost none of the blankets, at least," he said. "Some firewood, but that is not too serious. Most of the cooking equipment has gone, and all but one bottle of water. I am sorry."

We were all surprised at his apology.

"It wasn't anyone's fault," said Mum. "Something

frightened her. I'm sure she wouldn't have fallen if she hadn't been badly scared."

"I saw it," I said.

Mum and Dad looked at me. The Guide added, "I too."

It was true. When I had glanced up to see what the donkey was looking at just as she jumped sideways, I'd caught a glimpse of a disappearing bushy tail, held low.

"Some kind of dog again," I said, checking across at the Guide with my eyes, for confirmation that he'd seen the same thing.

He nodded.

"And I'd just made that quip about your wolf bringing us another rabbit!" said Dad. "I bet it was the same one!"

"No, it couldn't have been," I said firmly, and they all looked questioningly at me, except perhaps the Guide, who looked as if he knew what I was going to say.

"Because the donkey saw my dog, or wolf, last

night. I think that's why *I* wasn't scared. Because *she* wasn't."

Mum and Dad didn't seem to know quite what to make of this, but looked over interestedly at the donkey, who just looked back at them rather blankly.

After this incident, the Guide walked in front of the donkey, to give her reassurance in case she saw anything scary again. I felt sorry for her. She kept well away from the edge now, but kept tilting her head to look up at the outcrop, just in case there was anything up there about to leap upon her.

In the end, she must have grown tired of twisting her neck, because she settled down to her normal way of going, and we made good progress, reaching the top of the pass just as night began to fall.

SEVEN

Just as the Guide had said, the path flattened out and disappeared at the top of the pass. The earth was hard and dry, and scattered with stones and boulders that had slipped down from the top of the mountain, but there was a patch of ground that looked beaten and trampled, with the gray ash of a dead fire in the center of it.

"Other travelers have stopped here," said Dad, noticing it. "A wilderness hotel."

"Many people have come through this way, to the border," agreed the Guide, unloading the donkey.

"There's not much for her to eat, up here," said Mum. The donkey, free now to wander, looked rather dejectedly around her, and then wandered up to the only bush—sticking out scraggily from the side of the outcrop—and started ripping off the leaves.

"She must have a cast-iron mouth," said Dad,

impressed, as the donkey battled calmly with the twigs and thorns.

"I'm pleased to say you were thoughtful enough to spare her last rations," smiled the Guide. "There's a handful left. And she knows it."

Sure enough, the donkey kept one eye on him, and hurried back to the packs as the Guide pulled out her bundle of dried grass.

"Can't see a drop of water, though," said Dad.

"She can manage a long time without," said the Guide, "long enough to cross the border, though she'll be pleased to have some then. It is we who have the problem, however."

This reminded everyone that we had run out of food, and had very little water as most had gone over the edge with the baggage Dad had had to cut away.

Mum started sorting through our remaining packs in a hopeful sort of way, and eventually pulled out two more sachets of powder, which were a salt and sugar mixture you could mix with water.

She sat back on her heels and looked at them in dismay.

"Not really a lot of use with only a couple of mouthfuls of water each. I don't know—do we want our water plain, or flavored?"

"It might be medically advisable to use that stuff, but I'd like to keep it plain for some reason," said Dad, and we agreed. It didn't exactly taste bad with the sachets added, but not that good, either.

Dad started digging around in his own pack, and after a lot of fumbling around said, "Aha!" and pulled out a crumpled piece of silver foil.

"I saved four pieces for just such an emergency. From the food parcel Granny sent last month."

"Chocolate!" me and Mum shrieked.

The Guide smiled and then laughed at us as we clamored round Dad, but no amount of encouragement from us would persuade him to take his piece, so Mum and Dad gave me two.

Although we tried to suck and not chew it, it soon

melted and was gone, and then we had to have a swig of the valuable water to wash it from our dry mouths and throats.

Meanwhile, Dad had started to make the fire. He was good enough at it now, it seemed, to satisfy the Guide, because he let Dad get on with it and stopped hovering and helping, as he had done when Dad had first tried.

"I am not a hunter, just a guide," said the Guide, passing the water bottle back to Mum after his turn, "but I will just see if there isn't a rabbit. I don't know why there would be, with so little to eat up here, but the dogs we've seen must eat something."

And he dusted off his khaki shirt and trousers and set off, with the donkey watching after him, but seeming to know she wasn't supposed to follow.

While Dad fussed around the fire, poking in a twig here and there and blowing on it when it was going perfectly well, I checked on the Fish.

He seemed all right, but hung near the bottom,

looking smaller than I'd remembered and paler. Mum had tutted about the little plastic water bottle the first night we'd camped after transferring the Fish to it from the bowl.

"It's far from ideal," she'd complained. "Fish need a nice big open area on top to let in the air. The shape of this bottle does exactly the opposite. I would normally cut it down about halfway, but you can't carry it open like that. The water would come out as it sloshed about."

Finally, she'd had to make two tiny holes in the plastic top with a needle, and we'd jammed the bottle upright for carrying, among my clothes in the top of my backpack, so that the neck of it just stuck out from the flap into the air.

"Sorry, Fish, there goes your view," I'd said.

Whenever we'd settled for the night, I'd taken off the lid to try and let in more air, and just hoped no one would knock the bottle over. I always found the best rock I could to avoid this happening, and twitched and shouted, "Watch the Fish!" every time anyone went past it, until the grown-ups started mimicking me.

"What do you think?" I asked Mum as she came to inspect the bottle and its contents. "Do you think he'll make it?"

"How do you know it's a he?" she asked, staring at him.

"I don't. Actually, he looks as much like a she. I just don't like calling him 'it,' " I explained.

"Anyway, he, she or it is going to make it, I'm sure," she answered. "As the Guide said, none of this is ideal. We are just hanging on because things will be better soon."

"Does the Fish know things will be better soon, though? Maybe he—or she—won't really try, if he thinks he will always be stuck in that bottle?"

"Creatures are so tough," said Mum, "it's amazing what they'll put up with. Poor Fish was still trying to breathe in the mud puddle, wasn't he, when you pulled him out. Maybe thinking, It's worth it, more rain might come and fill this pond again—who can tell?"

"That's true," I said, "I do hope the Guide finds something to eat. I'm so hungry. I can't imagine walking tomorrow on no tea and no breakfast and no lunch."

Mum put her arms around my shoulders and gave them a big squeeze. She is small, as I told you, but has arms with an iron grip.

"But we will if we have to. And we can, can't we? Because we know the border is at the bottom of the mountain. And Dad can call a truck from the other aid workers to carry us to the camp. And there'll be food and water at the camp. And then—"

"*Then* we get to go on an airplane?" I asked hopefully. You have to remember, I was only small when I'd come to this country on a plane and couldn't really remember it. The idea was still pretty exciting to me.

Mum laughed.

"Yes, then, *then* we'll go on an airplane, back home. And we, at least, will be a bit more comfortable."

While we had been looking at the Fish and talking, night had come and gathered the sky, dark and cold, around us. There were a few stars, but the moon only shone as a grayish haze.

"Cloudy," said Dad, squinting up at the sky from where he crouched by the fire, rubbing his hands. "That's good. A clear night up on the top here would be even colder."

There was a silence for a moment, and I think we all thought about the Guide at the same time, because we would normally be eating by now, and we hoped he might find something. I saw the donkey pause in her chewing for a moment, and stare with pricked ears toward the direction the Guide had taken.

When we heard the sound of a footfall, we all looked up hopefully. But out of the gloom, not one, but three ghostly figures emerged.

Mum and Dad stood up and faced them straight-away, while I grabbed my Fish's bottle instinctively and clutched it to me.

The three men stopped just outside the circle of

light thrown by our fire. They were dressed in the normal, pale robes of villagers, but they clasped guns slung across their chests and had belts of bullets low around their hips. I suddenly realized that they looked as cautious as Mum and Dad.

There was silence for a moment while they took in the scene, and my parents stood there, looking ridiculously as if they were about to tell off someone they'd found wandering in their back garden. For a moment I felt a terrible urge to giggle rise up inside me, but I stared hard at the men's guns to frighten it back down again.

The first man, who had a bit more of a beard than the other two (which was maybe why he got to be in the lead), released his hold on his gun and let it swing, looking relieved, but puzzled. The two behind him, seeing this, did the same.

Dad spoke first, in a language he'd learnt before he came to the country, but which wasn't used by the local people. I only knew the language of the village— a dialect, Mum called it—so I didn't understand him, but I thought it sounded questioning, welcoming but firm all at the same time—a bit like a head teacher asking what a new kid is doing hanging around in the corridor, if you know what I mean.

The first man looked even more relieved and pleased, obviously because he understood Dad, and he prattled back at great speed. I could see Mum and Dad looking a bit perplexed and concentrating hard. They still found it difficult sometimes when people spoke quickly. Dad gave up trying to follow what the man was saying, rubbed his forehead and said to Mum, "He's speaking in another dialect, isn't he?"

At this point, a stocky, fierce-looking man stepped forward very confidently and, to my surprise, smiled at my parents, and said something to the first man, who stopped talking. Then Stocky grinned at my parents again and said something else, and Mum and Dad smiled much more cheerfully and said something back, and I realized that they recognized each other.

"I tell him, you come from the village, I know you there. You help with the school and the medicine," he said. There was general greeting all round, but still I noticed a certain guarded tension in the air. The third, youngest man stood looking slightly bored and not particularly friendly.

The first man, with the biggest beard, whom I called Leader in my head, tried our language, less confidently than Stocky.

"You are aid workers. You have food, water."

I think he meant these to be questions, but he spoke as if he were stating facts.

"We have no food. We did not bring enough for this journey. We thought we could cross on the road. We did not expect to have to cross the mountains, but they closed the border," answered Dad.

It was confusing to listen to, because as he spoke, so did Stocky, translating what he said into Leader's language, so that he could understand.

Dad went on, "We lost most of the water. The donkey went over the edge and I had to cut away the packs to get her back up."

The older man sighed and shook his head, whether

in sympathy for us, or disappointment that we had no supplies to share, I couldn't tell.

The youngest man, who hadn't shown much interest so far, suddenly looked across at me, still huddled by the rock on which the Fish's bottle had stood. He said something sulkily to the others, and they too turned to look at me as if they'd only just noticed I was there.

A frown passed over Stocky's face. "He says, what has the child got there?" he explained apologetically to my mother. "He says, it looks like water." Then he turned and said something sharply to the youngest man.

Leader approached me and Mum said, "It's all right, Tiger, show him your bottle," in a bright kind of way which I knew was put on.

Slowly, I pulled the bottle from my chest, where I had tried to hide it, and reluctantly held it up in the light of the fire. Leader approached, curious, and asked a question in his own language.

Mum said, "That is just a fish. The child saved it from a mud puddle when we left, and carries it. There is not much water in the bottle. And it would taste bad, I think."

"Yes, indeed!" said Leader, in our language, and to my surprise, laughed suddenly, but in a nice way, not *at* me, and ruffled my hair. Then there was a lot of talking between the men, who looked at me and pointed as they did so.

"They think it's strange, what you're doing, but they are impressed," Dad said to me, looking surprised himself. "They say, good for you, well done."

I think we'd all been thinking of the Guide, in between, and at first had wondered where he was, and hoped he'd come back soon. But now we were hoping he wouldn't, if he had a rabbit or something. A rabbit hadn't gone far between four of us, and we had the feeling that these men, however friendly they seemed, might take it.

The Guide was clever. Perhaps he was watching, and waiting for the men to go.

But at that moment, the donkey, who had watched all the goings-on for a while before tucking into her dried grass again, looked up for the second time that night and pricked her ears in the direction from which the men had come.

The older man noticed—obviously he brought more to his job as leader than a bigger beard—and grabbed hold of his gun again and turned around. The other men immediately did the same.

"It's all right, it's all right, it's just our Guide," said Mum and Dad together, stepping toward them, and Stocky said something to the other two, presumably repeating what they were saying, but they all remained with their guns pointing in the direction of the donkey's stare. She gave a little wheezy greeting, hardly a bray, as we saw the Guide materialize, then pause. He said something, in a very calm voice, and the guns were lowered again.

The men drew aside to let him pass through them and join my anxious parents by the fire. He had something swinging in his hand, but it was something earthy, and looked like a lump of old wood, not a rabbit.

Dad introduced him, using the Guide's proper name, which I could not pronounce, and the men immediately looked suspicious again.

"That cannot be," explained Stocky, as if Dad had made some mistake. "This name, the whole family were killed."

There was more talk between the men, while the Guide stood quietly, saying nothing.

Leader asked him something, and the Guide simply said his own name again, insistently, and looked at them all calmly.

Then the youngest one said something firmly and stepped forward into the firelight, near the Guide, as if he would put an end to all this nonsense.

Stocky said to my parents, "He says he knew the family well. He would know."

Silence fell. The fire did not seem to crackle, and the donkey stood soundless and unmoving as a statue.

The bored-looking young man stared deep into the face of the Guide, doubtfully, and said something brief, dismissive. I noticed his hand was resting on his rifle again, and his fingers stayed close to the trigger.

The Guide looked as deeply back into the eyes of the other, and gently said something that might have been the young man's name and then what sounded like a question.

How can the Guide talk to a man with a gun in that way—as if he were speaking to a frightened child? I thought. If he tries to shoot the Guide, I thought, I will dive for his legs. I will thump and bite and scratch. . . .

In the white-orange glow of the fire, we saw the young man's face change. Miraculously, it changed.

From blank and bored, his face now showed a bewildering range of emotions. Have you ever watched the shadows of clouds when they race across the land in the sun? That's what it was like, seeing his expression change, every part of a second. Incredulous, wondering, relieved, sad, confused, happy. For a moment, he seemed speechless. When at last he spoke, his voice came out dry and shaky, and he only seemed to say one word. I wished I understood.

He made as if to throw his arms around the Guide, then suddenly seemed to change his mind and dropped them by his sides and backed away.

Leader looked at him as if he had gone mad, and asked him something sharply. The other answered in a low voice, still seeming shocked and unable to take his eyes from the Guide, who smiled rather sadly, saying nothing.

Stocky said quietly to us, "He says, he was a good man. No, now he says, he *is* a good man. I don't know what's got into him."

Leader looked exasperatedly at his men, then glanced at the earthy thing in the Guide's hand and muttered in a grumpy way. Stocky said, "He says, if you're going to eat *that*, you definitely don't have anything else. He is sorry if we have disturbed you."

With that, there was a rapid goodbye, especially from the young man who had looked bored, but now just looked slightly frightened, and the three left.

We all looked at each other, especially at the Guide, who tried to act as if nothing unusual had happened, but sat down on a rock near the fire and started scraping at the earthy lump he'd brought, with his knife. I eyed it with suspicion. What did the men mean, we obviously had nothing else to eat or we wouldn't be eating *that*?

The Guide felt my eyes upon him.

"It's a root. I would normally boil it, but there isn't enough water. We have to cook it in the fire, and it will take a long time. Don't worry, it doesn't taste bad. It just doesn't taste of much, that's all."

"Thank you, thank you for finding anything at all," said Mum quickly, throwing me one of her looks.

I didn't want to seem ungrateful.

"Yes, thank you, I *am* hungry," I said.

Dad squatted down next to the Guide and picked at the bits he was shaving off the lump.

Quietly he asked, "What was the matter with that man?"

"My family died, he believes I am dead too. All this

time. I went away for a while, he has not seen me, why should he think otherwise? He was pleased to see me, I think." He spoke in a matter-of-fact way. He kept his head down, concentrating on his work, so did not notice Dad looking across the fire at me and Mum.

We were all thinking the same thing. Pleased, maybe, but also afraid. Why?

However, none of us was going to be impolite enough to carry on discussing something that the Guide obviously didn't want to talk about, and with the men's departure relief washed over us and made us realize that we were all very tired.

I carefully put my Fish, in his bottle, on the rock again, and snuggled down inside my blankets. The root would take ages to cook, said Mum, so we might as well sleep a little and wake and eat it when it was ready. "Like a midnight feast!" she said cheerfully.

EIGHT

Nothing eventful happened that night. Being woken up in the middle of it to eat a strange, baked root might seem unusual in the normal run of things, but after our adventures it was just another irritation.

The Guide had been right—the root didn't taste unpleasant, it just didn't taste of much at all. I would say, it tasted like boiled potato with nothing to flavor it, but had the texture of a rather gluey carrot. But then it made you realize how much taste a potato really has.

I had treated potatoes badly. I had argued with Mum about finishing them up. Now I imagined the taste and it seemed wonderful. I swore if she gave me a big plate of them when we got out of this, I would eat every last one and never complain again.

Just to add a little spice to the meal, there were bits of bonfire stuck over the root. The Guide laughed at

126

me as he saw me trying to pick off the specks of black, and spit them out when they crunched in my teeth.

"Good for the stomach," he said. "Makes sure you don't have an ache from eating the root."

I didn't know about that. I reckoned I was going to wake the next morning with the same dull ache I'd had for days. The only good thing about hunger is, you can't tell if you've got indigestion.

As I dropped back to sleep that night, I listened to Dad and the Guide murmuring away in their deep, low voices. It was a comfortable sound to hear as you drifted off, I thought, and suddenly realized that I would miss it when this journey was over, if nothing else.

But tonight, something the Guide said left me with an uncomfortable feeling.

Dad said, "Well, that's the last we'll see of those men, I expect. They seemed a bit—" I don't know if he was going to say "scared" or "disappointed" because the Guide interrupted.

"I wouldn't be so sure of that, not that you should worry unduly," he said slowly.

"Why would they bother with us, now they know we haven't got anything?" Dad asked, with a note of uncertainty in his voice.

"There are rumors—I admit I did not say earlier—the guards at the border told me when they could not let us pass—but there was nothing to be done, so no point in frightening anyone. . . ."

I'd never heard the Guide sound so awkward and it was obviously as disturbing to Dad as it was me. I heard him sit up abruptly.

"*What*, for Heaven's sake?"

The Guide made a shushing sound because my dad's voice had got louder. I made sure I looked very asleep.

After a pause, the Guide continued.

"Some of the mountain men are looking out for hostages—but they need ones from the right countries, to use as a lever on those countries to intervene, perhaps, in the fighting. I felt these men were just checking. You might be valuable. We must stay close together and keep our eyes open from now on."

"Oh no," Dad groaned, and I heard him slump back on the cold ground. "What do you propose? I mean, we haven't any weapons."

"Stick with me. I know these mountains" was all the Guide said.

I thought I would never get to sleep, but the stab of worry in my stomach just melted in with the general ache, and my body was so tired that sleep must have taken over, so before I knew it, it was morning.

I yawned and rubbed the sleep out of my eyes—no washing now for days, because of the water—and screwed the top back on the Fish's bottle. He circled around a few times.

"At least your eyes aren't gritty," I told him, "and I'm sorry if you're hungry, but you didn't miss anything by not sharing tea last night."

Dad gave my bottom a shove with his foot as he passed, carrying a pack to the donkey.

"Stop grumbling, grouch," he said, grinning, "by nightfall we'll be over the border."

He whistled around cheerfully, and his mood was

infectious. I put the worry of what I'd heard out of my mind. Me and Mum stamped out the fire and rolled up the last blankets with more energy than we thought we had. The Guide, however, still had his serious face on.

Dad went over, as he did every morning, to pretend to help the Guide load the donkey. What he really did was stand watching, while rubbing the donkey's long ears, and scratching between her eyes, and talking to her.

"Soon be over," he told her, "and you can have a rest. Do you think it will be straightforward enough, going down?"

The Guide never seemed to be confused as to when Dad was speaking to the donkey, or speaking to him.

"I have always said, it will not be easy," he answered. "You have seen all the way, how the earth has slipped. We do have a very narrow stream of mud to cross—we can almost jump it. After that, well, it is a little steeper on the way down, and I think we'll find that the path will have gone completely. But we will make it by nightfall, certainly. The end of the journey always seems the hardest, after all."

Those words were to stay with me throughout that last day.

Once prepared, we looked around for the path. We'd camped on the flattened-out area, where the path just petered out. Which direction?

The Guide, almost apologetically, led us to the edge, which dropped away in front of us.

"Down there?" asked Dad, incredulous.

The Guide pointed to the right-hand edge, the side where the donkey had nearly gone off the path.

"That way—the gorge. That way"—here he pointed to the left—"the very top of the mountain."

"*That* way," Dad interrupted him, pointing straight in front of us, off the edge of the flattened area, "down. OK, OK. We'll manage."

I looked over. There was a narrow path at first, and surprisingly, a few trees, scrub and bushes—almost a wood. The path reappeared further down, looking a bit boggy where it ran alongside a narrow ribbon of mud, which must have been a stream during the rains.

In the wall of the mountain, to one side of it, there were the black mouths of caves.

"Remember," said the Guide, looking very serious and fixing each one of us with his steady look, "if anything happens—stick together, stick with me."

I felt a bad feeling in my stomach again. I looked at Mum. It didn't seem right that she was the only one who didn't know about the men. I decided that it was up to the Guide and Dad to decide whom they told and whom they didn't. I shouldn't have been listening anyway. For all I knew, Mum had been listening too—not much got past her, in my experience.

We set off down the path, the Guide, then the donkey, Mum, me and Dad, in that order. We had only taken a few paces when it happened. There was a terrible sharp crack sound, then another, and a whistling sound passed my shoulder and ear.

What happened next was all panic and confusion. I remember turning and looking up at the mountain above us and seeing a man there outlined black against the sky and rock behind him. He looked like one of the group who'd come to our camp.

Then someone knocked me down—I think it was Dad; he and the Guide were shouting, "Get down! Get down!"

Once down, I think we all realized that we were in trouble. The man and at least two others were running toward us, and lying on the ground seemed a bad idea to me. I wrestled Dad's arm out of the way as he also got to his feet and saw the men practically on top of us, guns in hands. In sheer panic I dived into the bushes and trees on the left and ran through and under them, half blinded, with twigs whipping my eyes, until I thought that they might follow the crashing sound I was making, so I stopped, and wriggled right into the middle of a practically dead bush, where I could pull my knees up in the dark and was fairly sure I couldn't be seen.

You have played chase and hide-and-seek games, like me. I knew enough, then, to remember to gasp *quietly*. After a moment or two, though, when I didn't hear the men's feet coming, I was horrified to find I was going to cry. It must have been because I didn't know what had happened to Mum and Dad. I bit my lip very hard and pinched some skin on my arm and held on tight to it until the feeling passed, because if I cried, someone was bound to hear me.

After a while, I breathed more easily and wiped my eyes—biting my lip had made them run anyway. I listened. There was complete silence. Why this seemed more terrible than the sound of running, shouting, or gunfire, I don't know, but it did. I sat and I waited for a very long time, and slowly, slowly, I felt cold, although it wasn't, really, and my teeth began to chatter.

I tried to make them stop because of the noise they seemed to be making, but they wouldn't. That decided me. I ought to move.

Very slowly, I unwound my legs, which had gone dead, and slithered out of the bush. My knees had stiffened and hurt as they took my weight and I straightened up. I realized then I must have been in the bush for a lot longer than I'd thought.

I started to walk—among the trees still, and keeping hidden, away from the path. I admit, I was very, very scared. If the grown-ups had been all right, they would be out there now, calling me. There was no sound.

I put each foot down silently, carefully. I had played this game with friends and it was important not to make two stones clack together, or a twig snap. It had seemed like life and death when you were playing. Now it really was. In a flash, I looked back at the Tiger from only days ago, and realized how young I had been. I was cross with that silly little child, but suddenly sorry, too, that *that* Tiger had gone forever. I swallowed a big lump in my throat for the second time, and concentrated on where I was going.

With every nerve and muscle tight like a bowstring, it only took a bird launching itself from a tree nearby to send me rushing into a panic again. I was near a small hole, not big enough to be called a cave mouth, in the side of the outcrop, and I flattened down and wormed my way in.

Once inside, I lay and listened and tried to pull myself together. Even then, I was sure it was men I had heard, crashing through the trees. I decided to carry on along the passage as I would be safer there than outside.

It was dark and cool, even cold, but once my eyes got used to it there was somehow enough light to see. Surely that meant it had to open out somewhere ahead?

The last part was quite hard to crawl along like a caterpillar, because your backside hit the ceiling as you pulled your knees underneath you to shove forward again. Every so often my backpack, which I'd forgotten about, would catch on the ceiling. I heard Fish's water glooping about from time to time, and wondered what he thought of all this, as his little world turned dark and chaotic.

Suddenly I came to an opening at the end, held on to the sides, and lowered my legs onto a convenient ledge. I was out of the passage, and into a large cave, but high up on a ledge. It was just possible I could jump down and land without hurting myself, but that wasn't what was worrying me.

The cave had obviously been lived in, and recently. There were the remains of a campfire in the middle and goatskins around on the floor. I started to think about crawling back down the tunnel, but at that moment angry voices, men's voices, froze me to the spot. They were walking right into the cave, arguing, and it was too late to move.

I was perched sideways on the ledge opposite and above them, with the narrow hole of the tunnel behind me offering the only hiding place. If I moved, though, there was no way they could miss seeing me, and I couldn't make it back down the tunnel quickly enough—they would be waiting at either end for me to come out. Unable to move anywhere, I stayed rigid and silent, with my toes and fingers touching the sandy ledge, and my knees almost on my chin. I told myself that, unbelievable as it might seem, they might not look up and notice me.

As they paced around the ashes of the fire, waving

their arms about and discussing fiercely, I recognized them as the men who had visited us. Though I couldn't follow what they were saying, it became clear that the one I'd nicknamed Stocky was picking on the young man who had seemed so uneasy about the Guide.

The younger man said little, but, with the same scared eyes of the night of the visit, firmly kept repeating something and putting his hands up in front of him, shaking his head in a way that clearly enough said "No way."

Leader, with his impressive beard, was saying very little, shaking his head now and then as if tired of the younger man. He said something briefly in a pause, and the argument seemed to die down for a moment.

Now I looked at Stocky, his back to the light coming in through the cave mouth, I recognized him as the man who'd opened fire on us. The same man who had smiled so much at my parents, and said what wonderful work they'd done. A chill ran through me and I felt pins and needles in my legs. I felt I would have to move soon, or I'd be stuck like this forever.

Just then, he stirred the ashes of the campfire with his foot in a cross way, and I saw that it wasn't quite out. It came to life with a soft red glow, and a waft of smoke drifted up toward me with the gorgeous smell of some kind of roasted meat. I could see a few burnt bits of bone on the edge of the embers, their leftovers from breakfast. They'd obviously had plenty to eat after all.

I was just thinking that they had been lucky getting away with a fire in a cave like that without anything like a chimney to take the smoke away, when I had a new and terrible problem to deal with.

My mouth started to water and my poor stomach, hungry as ever, came to life and let out a loud, rumbling gurgle. Horrified, I stiffened all over. None of them appeared to have heard it. They continued moodily staring at the fire and saying nothing. I willed them to start arguing again. You will know, if you have ever had a rumbling stomach, that there's nothing you can do to stop it.

Again, my stomach growled—this time, surely they would hear it.

In fact, the youngest man looked around, but luckily behind him, at the mouth of the cave, and said something that might have been "What was that?"

That was all it took for Stocky to start having a go at him again—I guessed it went along the lines of him being scared of everything and imagining things.

Then Leader stood up and spoke low and menacingly to the youngest man, who, to my surprise, began to get very agitated and shout back, flinging his arms about.

The echo of his voice bounced and crashed around the cave walls as I cowered on the ledge—Stocky began to shout too, till all the echoes met each other and made a booming that seemed to hum between my ears, and make my heart in my chest shake with the vibration. Just when it seemed unbearable and I thought if I didn't get out of there, I'd fall, there was a tremendous blast that thumped through my skull.

I opened my eyes; to my surprise, the roof of the cave was still there, and I was still on the ledge. But the youngest man was doubled over, clutching his side. I saw the sunset glow from the fire streak along the barrel of a gun that Stocky was lowering from his hip, and realized that he had shot the younger man.

The injured man turned in a flash and ran, staggering out of the cave mouth. Leader, who seemed almost bored by the whole business, said something to Stocky, and they hurried out too. Now was my chance, I decided. I had to get out. They could be back any moment.

I tried to haul myself back into the hole, but found my arms had no strength left and I could barely straighten my legs. Again I tried, but just could not lift myself.

With no choice, I sat on the ledge, looked down, and making sure I missed the fire, pushed off.

As I'd expected, my useless legs buckled on impact and I rolled over and over on a floor that had looked sandy from above, but that just about every part of my body told me was in fact very rocky. There was no time to check Fish's bottle. I trusted and somehow felt that it would be OK.

I bolted for the cave mouth and darted through it, fear now making my legs work instead of freezing them. I didn't know where I was going, but I turned instinctively in the direction opposite to the one the men had taken.

Only a few paces on, I heard a shout, and glancing back over my shoulder, saw Leader looking behind him and straight at me. I hurtled on, along a path that led steeply downward through scrub and trees, trying hard not to fall over my own feet.

Because the path twisted and turned, I could hear them following, but knew they lost sight of me from time to time. What to do? Come off the path and hide in the scrub? It didn't look thick enough to hide a dog. Outrun them? Where to?

I knew I couldn't run for long, but I put all my effort into a final sprint. If I could get distance between us, I might have a moment to hide—somewhere. I turned a corner and there—in front of me—was the narrow mud-stream. I sized it up in a moment. It was about four feet across, and normally I might have jumped and cleared it, but I had just used my last ounce of energy in the final sprint. Cramp was seizing every muscle in both legs.

I also saw that the other side was clear and open—if I made the jump, I'd be right out in front of them and they could just stand and shoot. Don't ask me what I was thinking of, or how the idea came to me. It didn't—I just—well, jumped straight into the mud.

I went down slowly at first, and I remember having time to think. It's an odd situation to find yourself willing yourself to sink faster, faster.

Down, down I went, and just as the mud came up to my ears, I reminded myself to take a big breath, and imagine I was swimming, or going under the bathwater.

The most terrifying moment was as I saw the surface of the mud stretching out from the bump on the middle of my nose and I shut my eyes and pulled my head under.

The mud was freezing and it wasn't like being underwater. You can shut your eyes underwater but it isn't the same dark as the blackness of closing your eyes under mud. You don't become instantly wet, like in water. Even under the surface, the terrible cold oozing and trickling carried on, as the mud rushed under my clothes, around the neck and armholes, crawling everywhere, as if searching out every part to take control.

I hung on to my dad's voice in my head, reading something out of a book of amazing facts, something about: "People can hold their breath for . . ." What was it? Three minutes? Three minutes, I told myself, whether it was true or not. Three minutes would surely do. It was the best anyone could do.

The blackness and the cold and the complete silence were starting to terrify me. "Pearl divers, however . . . ," continued my dad's voice. I forgot the rest, but struggled desperately to remember. That was it! I couldn't remember how long they could hold their breath, but anyway, they could go deeper underwater and hold their breath longer than anyone. I found myself thinking that I didn't need to know how long as I couldn't have timed myself with a watch if I had one, as I wasn't going to be able to look at it right now. At first, that made me want to giggle, but then I was scared I was going mad, so I gave myself a little shake.

My feet had hit the bottom, I realized with relief. That was something, at least. The mud settled and held me very firmly. I could be a pearl diver, with practice, with believing in it, I thought.

But slowly, surely, my chest started to ache and a pulse pounded in my head and I knew I had to get up to the surface again for air. I tried to imagine the men running up to the edge and wondering where I had gone. How long would they stand around and wait? Maybe they would have a lengthy argument again. Surely they'd take the path along to the right? But maybe they had seen the movement in the mud— they'd know what I'd done.

I put that out of my head. There was nothing else I could do now. My chest was bursting and I decided to let the air out, which would at least buy a second or two more time. It was like keeping yourself busy— something else to do.

I had worked out that I would do that, and then surface for air. But as I said, mud isn't like water. I blew the air out as slowly as I could as I started to paddle for the surface with my arms, but it was almost too hard to blow out through the sticky mud, which started to ooze in between my lips straightaway. For a moment I didn't move upward at all, and I thought my feet must have stuck in the mud forever and would hold me there until I died.

But the drought must have made the bed of the stream hard enough to be firm and solid, even under the mud, and a push with my knees meant I was slowly moving upward at last, pushing down with my hands and arms like the slowest, clumsiest bird you ever saw.

The hardest part was pulling my arms up against the mud for another push down, and my backpack dragged painfully on my shoulders and seemed to weigh five times as much as before.

Suddenly I remembered Fish. I had rescued him from mud like this—what must it have seemed like to him to be sinking into it again? Then I remembered that the lid of his bottle would be screwed on tight, and that he was still breathing easy in his own element. The mud would be too thick to squeeze through those tiny pinprick holes. He would have coped much better than I. He would be fine, if I could just get out of this.

A frog-style kick with my legs and suddenly I felt no resistance on my arms, as they must have come out into the air above the mud. One more push down with them, and my head would be out.

As my face broke the surface, I opened my mouth and dragged in a great gulp of air. I couldn't see a thing, and mud was between my teeth, over my tongue. Somehow I flailed, blind, toward the bank, got my hands on it and felt my feet firm on the stream's bed again, at the shallow edge.

The terror of not seeing, now, was everything. Were they standing there, guns aimed? Would I hear a shot and then it would all be over, without seeing anything? Would they stand there and wait for me to get out and just take me captive? Eyes still tight shut against the mud I could feel streaming down my face, I scraped the backs of my hands over the sparse grass I could feel on the bank, then pulled my fists over my eyelids.

When it seemed I'd cleared away enough of the mud, I opened them. Everything was blurry and my lashes were still caked, so I looked out on a world fringed brown at the edges.

The first thing I saw was some type of rough material, right in front of my nose. I couldn't make sense of that at all, so I looked up and slightly beyond it, then stiffened. There were the two men—Leader and Stocky. They were looking straight at me.

It was all over, then. It was almost a relief. I wanted to say, "All right, here I am." But I didn't. For some reason I just stood there in the mud still, and waited.

It all seemed strangely calm. They spoke quietly to each other in a bored way, as if they'd finished a job, and to my surprise, started to turn and walk away. It hit me suddenly. They hadn't seen me!

As they disappeared along the path, I looked again at the rough material almost against my nose on the bank. My eyes were clearing. I looked along it—it was something about the size of a large tree trunk. It must have blocked their view of me as I surfaced.

Slowly, slowly, I realized the fabric was clothing. Slowly, slowly, not wanting to look, I saw feet at the end further away from me, and turning my eyes unwillingly to the end of the shape nearest to me, I saw dark, curly hair, the back of someone's head. It was the body of a man, lying with its back to me along the bank.

Though it was further to wade to the end with the feet, fear made me choose that way. Clinging to the bank and going crabwise, I made it as far as I thought I'd need, past the feet, to be able to get out without touching it.

Painfully I dragged myself out of the mud and crawled on all fours a little way across the path. I don't know why, but I seemed to have lost all fear of the men, and didn't think about them returning. I peeled off the backpack and set it upright. It looked like part of a brown statue. I wiped a finger over Fish's bottle, to make him a window, and saw him dart and flash behind it for a moment. Like a dog drying itself, I scraped myself over the ground and rough grass, anywhere, to get the worst of the mud off.

Then, when I was ready, I sat down and faced the dead man.

It was, of course, the youngest man, who'd been shot. It wasn't as scary, or as bad as I thought, to look at him. He had a nice face, and he just looked peacefully asleep. There was a terrible dark stain on the side of his clothes nearest the ground, but you didn't really notice if you didn't look at it. And I decided not to.

I must have sat there for a long time, but I didn't notice that either. I felt lots of things that are hard to put into words. I wondered if he knew he'd helped save me, even though he was dead. I was angry with the other man for shooting him. And for just leaving him here like he wasn't worth anything. I sat there and felt that somehow I was keeping him company. None of this makes any sense, I know, but maybe my head was a bit mixed up from being in the mud and everything.

Then suddenly something changed, and I felt I didn't need to be there anymore. He was gone, after all, and there was just a useless body. And at exactly that moment, Mum, Dad and the Guide appeared from the path to the right of me, and Mum rushed up, but I couldn't stand up or even look pleased, I just sat with my arms around my legs, and my forehead on my knees, and started crying for no good reason, just when people could see me.

I managed to stop fairly quickly when they all put their arms round me, but then I started to shudder and shake and couldn't talk and tell them what had happened because my teeth were chattering too much.

They were very good, and didn't ask questions or tell me off for running the wrong way in the first place, like you'd expect grown-ups to.

One of them got a blanket from somewhere and put it round my shoulders as I was shaking so much, and Mum said, "It's the shock," and I managed to stop my teeth clanking together long enough to say, "What shock? I'm freezing because the mud was so cold."

Then Mum and the Guide started to rub me all over with the blanket, which was very rough and hairy, so it did work really well at getting off the mud and warming me up. I wondered why Dad wasn't helping and looked across at him sitting next to me and was shocked to see he was *crying*—my dad—crying!

"Dad! Please don't!" was all I could think to say. He was very quiet about it, I will say—but still. Then I felt guilty, I don't know why, and said, "I'm sorry, Dad. But I'm all right."

"No, no, Tiger. It's not your fault. It's all mine. I'm just—it's just happiness, you know, like women do at weddings sometimes."

I didn't know. I'd never been to a wedding. I looked at him doubtfully. The Guide touched his shoulder.

"Come on, now," he said simply.

NINE

Like me, the adults seemed unhurried and calm now. The Guide stepped across the mud to the other bank, using a huge log that had fallen, and collected other bits of tree and wood, making a dam. Then Dad sort of passed me across and we took the path on the other side with no problems.

There, at the end of the path, stood the donkey, with her back to us. When she heard us coming she turned and gave a little wheezy bray of welcome. It was so good to see her, I had to run up and give her a hug, though I think it was the Guide she was pleased to see really.

"What happened to her when we all ran off?" I asked.

"Good as gold," said Dad. "She seemed to just tuck herself away somewhere, and popped back out when we did."

The path this side was clear of scrub, and wide, and we sat down at the edge where the mountain fell away again below us. Here we told our stories in quiet voices.

Mum and Dad had run in the same direction as the Guide, who had practically had to fight them both, by the sound of it, to stop them rushing off to find me while the armed men were still racing about looking for them. They had managed to remain hidden in the scrub until it was safe, and had then started to search. All of them were very cut about by thorns.

Looking for me at the mud-stream had been the Guide's idea, because he knew that *I* knew we had to cross it. He thought that if I'd escaped—which he thought very likely—I would have sense enough to find my way there.

I was proud that he'd thought all this, but of course, my ending up there had nothing to do with sense and more to do with blind panic. They were kind enough not to say if they noticed this, when I told them my story.

"Ah," the Guide said, when I got to the part about

finding the youngest man dead. "He didn't agree with their plan, you see—and it doesn't suit these people to have one of their number turn against them."

"It doesn't seem right to leave him like that," put in Mum. "He was some mother's son, as they say." There was silence for a moment.

"And now," explained the Guide, looking at me carefully, "we must go on, and not give too much thought to these men anymore. I have asked some friends of mine, real soldiers, to look out for them and they are in pursuit. They will also," he added, turning toward Mum, "find and attend to that young man."

"We do have to finish this, Tiger," said Dad, tired, looking at me. "Are you ready?"

"Yes," agreed Mum, and stood up.

"OK," I said, feeling much, much stronger for a moment, now we were all back together. But I couldn't help looking around as I stood up.

The Guide noticed.

"We can't do this looking over our shoulders all the time, Tiger. You must trust, now. We have to get down the mountain and concentrate. What will be will be. We can only try our best, eh? And it is harder to catch a Tiger than those men thought, eh?" And he smiled suddenly, which he didn't do very often, and which always made anyone smile back however they felt.

We went to the edge and looked down.

There was no path, just loose rubble and bushes, some growing, some fallen. I had clambered down similar slopes, but not for such a long way. It wasn't a sheer drop, and every so often there was another outcrop, or more level area, where we could stop and catch our breath—or where you might end up if you slipped.

The Guide set off first, and the donkey braced her back legs on the edge and felt around with little tap-tapping movements of her front hooves. She seemed less worried than when she'd had to enter the mud, despite her earlier fall.

Seeing them upright, and moving downward, we all followed—me and Mum first and Dad behind. We told him not to fall, because we didn't like the idea of him landing on top of us.

At first, we could almost walk in a normal way, especially as areas of path would suddenly appear from out of the rubble. The Guide obviously knew the way very well, because he led us across the featureless piles of stone and earth, tracking exactly where the path must have been. Where it reemerged it was a relief, even for a few paces, to stride along.

But increasingly you had to walk sideways, trying to keep a grip with your back foot, while your front foot slithered. Loose rock scuttled away with every step, and showered down the mountain. Dad's heavy feet sent earth and stones onto me and Mum, so he hung back a little.

In the tricky bits, it seemed to take hours to go a few paces. The only good thing about the occasional, scary slither was that you covered the ground very quickly.

None of us said anything, because we were concentrating.

Dad, from his vantage point above and behind us, called out once, "Watch the Guide. Follow him exactly. He knows what he's doing."

We realized that it was too easy to end up staring at your own feet. Not only did this take you slightly off course, but you missed the handy tips the Guide passed on in the route he chose—for example, he had a knack of noticing where a bush would hold the ground well with its roots, and of keeping handholds nearby, such as roots and even tussocks of grass.

By midday, we had been walking and sliding for almost six hours. Without a word between us we kept our eyes on the only level place ahead, where an outcrop jutted out horizontally with a few bushes to mark it, and knew we would rest when we reached it.

The donkey, who had overtaken the Guide at some point, got there first and obviously had the same idea. She stopped immediately and started picking at the bushes in a determined manner.

The Guide and Mum reached it next, and I slipped, went down on my bottom, and arrived sitting down rather suddenly, so Mum had to hop out of the way. Luckily, seeing this, Dad picked his way very carefully for the last few feet. A tobogganing man might have sent the lot of us, donkey and all, over the edge of the outcrop, in spite of the bushes.

I stayed sitting down, getting my breath back, and Mum and Dad hovered around for a moment as if looking for a rock to sit on. There weren't any, except a few jagged ones, so they sort of crumpled where they stood and sat hugging their knees with their heads down.

The Guide straightened the donkey's packs before sitting down next to me. For once, I had nothing to say. I didn't even seem to be able to think, I was so tired. The Guide leaned back to look at my backpack.

"Fish still there," he said, as if to cheer me up.

I had almost forgotten the Fish, after my slide. Guiltily, I slipped off the backpack. It wasn't really heavy, but it suddenly seemed very difficult to pull it around onto my lap. I took out the bottle and surveyed the Fish. Small and pale—such a fuss I had made about such a little thing.

I examined him closely. The fins, almost transparent, had tiny lines radiating outward. They were all placed just so. The tail spread upward and downward, forked in the middle, the tips tapered just right. Looking very closely, you could make out the tiny scales all over. Each one fitted snugly over the next. The eye was big and golden, with tawny mottling, and a black pupil right in the middle. He was perfect. I forgot how small and dull he seemed to have become, and felt a warm glow run through me. I was very glad I had saved him and he was still with us.

"So small, so delicate, but so tough," said the Guide, looking with me, and giving me one of his rare smiles.

It was the dullest, quietest and saddest rest we'd had so far. Usually, we didn't exactly celebrate, but we cheered up at these points. This time there was no reward of a little food. The only reward we could offer ourselves was simply to stop for a while.

Mum passed around the water bottle. We had been rationing it, but now it was obvious that there was not enough left to save. There was one gulp each left. For some reason, I didn't much care. I didn't really feel thirsty anymore, and not even hungry. I was used to the dull ache in my stomach now, and it almost made you feel *not* like eating.

The Guide was looking at my sandals. "The feet are rubbing again," he said to my mother, looking across at her.

She lifted her head and looked at him for a moment as if she had been daydreaming, and didn't understand.

"Have you any cloth?" asked the Guide, more insistently.

Mum gave herself a little shake, and turned to her bag uncertainly. Dad seemed to wake up a bit too and said to her, "No, it's OK. I've a spare T-shirt here."

He pulled one (which looked as if it had once been white) out of his bag, and asked the Guide for his knife.

Having made a cut to start with, he managed to tear it into strips like thin bandages, sometimes using his teeth. Hardly bothering to stand up, he shuffled over to me and inspected my feet and the sandals.

I hoped he wasn't going to suggest bandaging my feet

again. He was too tired and it would be too dangerous to try and carry me down the mountain. I had seen even the donkey struggling to keep her feet. I didn't think I'd be safe on her back, and especially not half on her neck, in front of the packs, pointing downhill.

But Dad had a good idea. We pulled off the sandals, and Dad carefully bound around the straps with the strips of T-shirt. They were tighter, but softer, when I put them back on, and I could do them up a bit more loosely so that they weren't *too* tight.

"Is that better?" asked Mum.

"Yes," I said, "but I hadn't really noticed they were sore this time."

Dad straightened up and looked down at me, then looked at the Guide.

"How much further?" he asked.

"Just under the same time again, the same we have traveled already today," said the Guide firmly, getting to his feet.

"Last bit now," said Dad, seemingly to all of us. Me and Mum didn't move for a moment.

Dad went over to the donkey and put his arm around her head from underneath and steered her gently away from the bush, as if to point out that we were leaving.

So, slowly, me and Mum stood up again. I saw the empty water bottle on the ground near a rock, but Mum didn't pick it up in her tidy way like she would normally have done. She was too tired to care anymore.

The donkey obediently stopped eating and stood with Dad, but waited for the Guide to start off before following. Soon she overtook him again, picking her way slowly and carefully.

On and on we went, down and down. Sometimes we seemed to be traveling across the side of the mountain, which was easier going, but took us no closer to the bottom.

Then there would be another steep, crumbling descent and we would feel we were getting closer. Now the scrub was clearing, we could see the last hummocks at the base of the mountain, not foothills, just heaps of rock and gravel like at a quarry. They almost entirely obscured the road that marked the border, but we could just make it out.

Our journey went on like that for hours without change. Your body became tired with the effort of balancing and stumbling. The palms of your hands became laced with deep little cuts from the jagged, unforgiving stones that met you when you fell, or tried to hang on. Your brain and eyes became tired with the effort of looking, thinking, concentrating.

Once, the donkey slipped, and stopped, and her back end traveled right round her in a semicircle until she ended up facing the other way around, her head pointing up the mountain.

But she stood very calmly as the Guide slipped and staggered over to her, and somehow between them she ended up the right way around again, and they carried on.

Soon, time meant nothing. It was like being in the mud. I had started to accept that I would forever be picking my way over this stone, around that tussock, falling, sliding, moving on again. Maybe I always *had* been. Maybe it would only end when I fell down and couldn't get up anymore. I forgot, or was too tired, to think of anything else, anything that had happened before, anything that would happen.

Little snippets of our journey—the cooking pot falling into the mud, the donkey hanging over the edge, the strange men's faces gleaming in the light of our fire—flitted in and out of my mind, but I was no longer sure if they were all part of a dream, or if I was dreaming now.

Suddenly, Dad called out to the Guide.

I didn't hear what he said, but the Guide stopped, looked back at Dad, and then down and ahead of us again.

Mum, walking almost alongside me and a little in front, stopped too, so that Dad caught us up.

"A car," Dad said, panting. "A car on the road. I saw it."

I thought this should be good news, but I wasn't sure. He narrowed his eyes, and the Guide stopped and stared too.

"We have to go on, at any rate," said my mother, in a dull voice.

"I just hope—it could be anyone, I suppose," said Dad. "They can't send us back, now."

I didn't know what that meant. I couldn't make sense of it. I just knew, with certainty, that I couldn't go back. I could hardly go forward anymore.

The Guide must have come to the same conclusion as my mother, because he lowered his head to concentrate on the track again, and the donkey sighed and continued.

Under a lowering gray sky, we struggled up and over the last but one hillock of rubble before the road. I could dimly make out part of a car parked, its back end obscured by the last heap of shale. A man in some kind of uniform with a flat cap was standing with his hands resting on his hips, staring up at us.

As I started after Mum down the hillock, my legs finally crumpled, and I tumbled down, head over heels, and ended up, slightly winded, against a rock. Mum struggled to catch up with me. The Guide and donkey, hearing the start of my fall, stopped. I ended up almost on top of them.

I saw Mum stoop to pick something up as she approached me.

"Are you all right, Tiger?" she gasped urgently, short of breath. Seeing me nod and sit up, she leant over me and my rock to the donkey on the other side.

"Quick! Quick!" she said to the Guide. "Something, I don't know, anything!"

And then, in her hand, I saw it.

The Fish's little plastic bottle, hideously distorted, and opaque where it was sharply bent, was dripping water. There was a large crack and a small hole in one side near the base.

The Guide fumbled with the packs.

"There is nothing. We left the last water bottle," he said, desperately searching.

Then there was a scrape of metal, and Mum passed a baking tray we had used for cooking into my hands. It was blackened, greasy, and very shallow.

I was so weak, I could hardly hold it.

"Hold it flat and level," said Mum, almost crossly. "We are almost there. It is only a few more yards. Oh," she added almost tearfully, "there is no more water. He will only have what is left in the bottle."

She had the lid off the bottle and poured the poor Fish with his little pool of water into the flat tray. I struggled to stop it tipping.

The tray was bent, and where there were bumps and dents upward the water didn't even cover the base.

The Fish swirled into a corner, and I tried to keep the tray tilted a little that way.

"Mum, you are madder than me. How am I going to walk—"

I was going to say "holding this level?" but I just stopped. How was I going to walk at all? Despite the padding, my feet were cut to ribbons where tiny sharp stones had slipped between my sandals and my feet.

Besides, my legs wouldn't work.

"Pass it to me a moment," said the Guide, sharply, and leant across the rock and took the tray in a steady, straight grip; then, "Get up," he said, more fiercely than I had ever heard him before, "get up, stand up now."

To my own surprise, I did, and he passed the tray back to me.

"Keep it straight, keep it level. Mother, keep your eyes on Tiger's feet. Tiger, keep your eyes on the tray. Last few yards."

Mum and Dad, if they didn't like his sternness, didn't say anything.

Grimly, they steered me the first few paces and we reached the base of the hillock safely, behind the Guide and the donkey.

Up, over the next. Watching the water in the tray seemed to make me not notice the sharp stones, the tired feeling. Sometimes the water would slop away from the corner of the tray, taking the Fish with it. For a second he would lie stranded on one of the bumps, his gills flapping, in, out.

Then I would tilt the water back, like a tide coming in, and sweep the little Fish back into his safe corner, where the water just covered his top fin.

As we started down the last hillock, toward the

man in uniform who seemed to be waiting, watching us, the Guide said, "Border police. He is not supposed to let us pass."

Suddenly, there were black spots dancing in front of my eyes. I tried to blink them out of the way, so that I could see the Fish.

But the spots grew and grew in number, and started to collect together, so that I could hardly see anything but blackness. Again, my legs crumpled, and I fell.

This time, I heard the tray tumble, clanging away down the side of the hillock.

The Fish! Gone! This time gone forever!

Dad's arm was around the back of my neck and my shoulders, pushing me up into a sitting position.

"Come on, Tiger, come on. We're here. Sit up, quick, I have the Fish."

The surprise might have got rid of the black spots. I blinked and my eyes cleared.

I looked down at Dad's hand, curled in a gentle fist.

He opened his fingers to show me. There lay the

little Fish, looking paler and tinier than ever. The gills rose and fell.

"There's no water. He won't live," I said, starting to cry.

"In your mouth, quick. Shut up and stop crying."

"But . . ."

"I know a thing or two about fish, remember, Tiger? I used to go fishing. You just have to keep him wet. He will live, long enough." Dad said urgently, "In your mouth, now!" and I took the limp creature from his hand without another word, and slipped him into my mouth.

Gently, I pushed the little shape into my cheek. I sat up, and then stood.

Mum and the Guide were staring, concerned, but the Guide reached out and squeezed my hand before walking on ahead with the donkey again, and Mum now held my elbow tightly, so I couldn't fall again.

Dad overtook us and reached the uniformed man just after the Guide. As Mum and I drew closer, I could see he had a gun—not a long rifle, like the men in the mountains, but a shorter, heavier one, in a proper black holster. But I saw that he didn't move to take it out.

The Guide spoke to him and the policeman nodded and looked past him to Dad and then beyond, to me and Mum picking our way slowly, very slowly, the last few steps.

Then the man said something to the Guide and smiled and looked sort of sad at the same time, and the Guide turned to us and smiled, but didn't look sad at all.

Dad must have heard what he'd said as well, because he shouted to us, "It's all right. It's all right. He won't stop us or send us back."

We were finally all together there, huddled around the car.

The policeman spoke our language. "What is your name, little one?" he asked.

"That is no little one," said the Guide sternly, and proudly it seemed. "That is a Tiger."

I was glad he answered for me. When I tried to move my mouth or tongue, the Fish would slip from his place in my cheek, and was so streamlined it felt as if at any moment he would shoot down my throat, and I would swallow before I knew what had happened. You will know what I mean if you have ever chewed a chewy sweet and tried to make it last as long as you can.

"I am supposed to stop anyone trying to cross the border," said the policeman, "but I am not stopping the wretched people I find. I am certainly not going to stop you. There are laws greater than the law of my land, others greater than the ruler of my land, whom I have to answer to."

Dad said, "Thank you, thank you so much. I know you are certainly not allowed to help those entering. But we are not local refugees. We are aid workers. We have an embassy in your capital. I wonder if you would make a call for us. . . ."

I sat down on the dusty road, and leant my back against the car's tire. I closed my eyes and smelt the hot smell of metal, of gasoline and oil. My head ached.

I felt Mum sit down alongside me and then take me in her arms and hug me.

"It's all right, Tiger. This country and our country are friends, and the policeman is sure he's allowed to help us. He's calling his bosses and the embassy right now."

Just at that moment, Dad touched my leg and I opened my eyes. "Come on, Tiger. He's giving us a lift in his car. Up you get, and hop in."

I should have been pleased, but I just felt irritable. Every time you sat down, or fell down, they made you get up again. And I couldn't swallow or speak very well.

"Water," I said, with difficulty, trying not to bite the little shape in my mouth. "Ask him, water first."

I heard a murmur, then the policeman said, "Of course, how stupid of me. You must be so thirsty."

He passed a big, clear plastic bottle to me, but I waved it away and said, "Others first."

He looked surprised, but all the grown-ups looked at me knowingly and took long swigs and gulps before passing it back. The Guide knew what was on my mind.

"Drink first, Tiger," he said, handing me the bottle.

I pushed the Fish firmly into my cheek with my tongue and tipped the bottle to my mouth. A thin trickle was all I allowed over my tongue, down my throat. Finally, I leant forward, wiggled with my tongue and slipped the Fish into the neck of the bottle.

"What . . . ? Are you all right?" asked the policeman, worried.

I held up the bottle to show him.

"It's a fish," I said. "I'm sorry, you can't have your bottle back, just yet."

And then I climbed into the backseat of the car, gripping the bottle, and Mum and Dad say I fainted, but I think I just fell instantly asleep.

TEN

I can just about remember waking up a little and it was dark, and someone was carrying me. We looked like we were at the refugee camp.

The next bit Mum says was a dream, but I still don't know.

I woke up in a nice, clean bed, very low to the ground, with white sheets on it. It was dark, so I knew it was still nighttime. I was in some kind of hut or building. There was a tube going from my arm into a clear bag full of what looked like water, hanging from a pole by the bed. I knew that was called a drip, because Dad had used them on some of the sick villagers.

On a chair next to my bed sat the Guide. He looked clean and fresh and someone must have given him new clothes, because his dusty old khaki shirt and trousers had gone and he was all in white.

"You look like a doctor," I said sleepily.

"Thank you," he said, with a big grin. "I am sorry I shouted at you, Tiger."

"You didn't shout at me," I said, "when?"

"Well, maybe not shouted. But I had to be stern with you, when we all wanted to carry you the last part really. But we couldn't. All of us were too weak. It was important you got up. It was good you made it on your own two feet."

"Oh, that's all right," I said. Nothing seemed to matter from the comfort of that bed. "My Fish . . ."

I looked around.

I couldn't see the bottle anywhere.

"Don't worry. Come, I will show you."

And I got out of bed and followed, wheeling the drip along, and we went out of the building and into the moonlight, and into another building. There were hundreds and hundreds, maybe thousands, of bottles, all different shapes and sizes, stacked on shelf after shelf. In each bottle, there was a little fish, some bigger, some smaller than mine.

"Your Fish is here, quite safe."

"But how will I know which—how do you know which is mine?" I asked, staring at all the bottles.

"Easy. You will always know, I will always know. How could we forget Fish?"

And the Guide reached out in the moonlight of the open door and picked out a bottle, and sure enough, it was the policeman's, and there was my Fish, swimming around, brighter and bigger somehow than before.

"What will I do with him, when I go?" I asked. "I know I was going to let him go, but I am scared. . . ."

"When you do not see him anymore, you do not know that he is all right, that he is still there, is that it?" asked the Guide.

I nodded.

"Your mother, when she is not around, does she no longer love you?" he asked.

"Of course she does," I answered.

"This love, can you see it?" he asked.

"No, of course not."

"But it is there. The same as hope," he said, gently. I thought for a moment and then nodded, surprised. The Guide made the most complicated things seem simple.

Then I don't remember very well going back to bed, but in the morning I woke up, and this time it was Mum sitting in the chair, instead of the Guide.

Next to my bed was the bottle, and the Fish, looking larger and brighter than ever, turning this way and that, as if impatient.

"Tiger! You're awake. How do you feel?" said Mum.

"Ab-so-lute-ly marvelous," I said, stretching as I did so. "Can I have this stupid drip thing off now?"

"Yes, I should think so. We just wanted to get some fluids into you, and you weren't in a condition to drink. The car from the embassy is coming any minute, to take us to the airport. The staff here agree with Dad that you should be fit to travel."

Dad turned up then, poking his head around the corner of the doorway, and coming in when he saw I was awake.

"All fit, Tiger?" he asked.

"Yes, I can't wait," I said, feeling strength running through me again. My tummy rumbled. "Ooh, I'm hungry!"

"Slap-up breakfast is on its way. When you've eaten it, I want you to hop out of that bed, *gently*, mind you."

To cut a long story short, a nurse came around, shooed my parents away, and took off the drip. Then she called to someone outside, and a man appeared with a tray of food—some kind of porridge, but nicer than before, and bread, and different bits of fruit, and a big glass of water.

I tucked in and finished the lot, and I didn't have to think about Dad's advice to get up gently, because I had to lie there for a while to let it all go down, and when I got up, it had to be slowly, because I felt like I had the weight of the food, *with* the tray *and* the glass, in my stomach.

Mum had put strange, clean clothes on the chair by the bed, so I got out of the white gown I seemed to be dressed in, and put them on saying, "Ouch, ouch," as the cuts on my hands and feet complained.

There was a pair of slippers, about a size too big, but I put those on as well. I decided I didn't care if people stared on the airplane. I was not going to put on those old sandals ever again.

Then Mum and Dad appeared, and I picked up my bottle and went out to meet the car. The policeman had come to see us off.

Dad, who seemed to be worried and distracted about something, suddenly looked at the bottle as if he had never seen it before.

"Tiger, what were you planning to do with Fish?"

"I don't know," I said. I had got in the habit of carrying him everywhere.

The grown-ups obviously thought I wanted him as a pet, and looked at each other. Mum said carefully to me, "I don't think he can live in our country, Tiger."

Dad said, "I don't think Customs will let him through, to be honest."

At that moment, the policeman stepped forward.

"I will take him, Tiger. I know a beautiful river. It never dries up, and no one even fishes there. He will be safe, I promise."

To everyone's surprise, I handed over the bottle. The Fish turned this way and that in the light. All the colors of the rainbow shone from his scales, and his underside flashed silver. He seemed almost too big to fit in the bottle, though it was so large.

"Oh, he is beautiful, and so big. How could he fit in your little mouth? How did he get through the neck of this bottle, even? I will cut the top off, to let him go. Well done—I can see why you saved him," said the policeman, admiring the Fish as he held the bottle up to the light, and everyone agreed, and I could see Mum and Dad looking puzzled, because they, like me, did not remember the Fish looking like that.

Dad still looked left and right, with a worried look, as the driver held the car door open for us.

"What's the matter?" I asked.

"The Guide," said Mum, "and the donkey. They just seemed to disappear last night. We would have just liked to say thank you and goodbye. They had to follow on foot, though it was only a short way, because the Guide wouldn't leave the donkey in order to ride with us in the car. No one seems to have seen them here."

"Oh," I said, surprised, "don't worry. The Guide was here last night. He was sitting by my bed. He had all new clean clothes on. He was fine."

Mum and Dad looked very surprised, but relieved.

"Are you sure?" they asked.

"Sure," I said firmly. "You don't have to see some-one to know they're all right and that they are there. He's around here, somewhere."

And I got in the car, and they got in too, and we headed off toward the airport.